"Hi," Sawyer Paxton said as he walked past us in the hall.

My heart beat in double time just to look at him. How could any one guy be so incredible-looking? He had on jeans and a red rugby shirt with a blue logo that matched the blue of his eyes. And it wasn't just that he was so cute. He was smart, too. And talented. And sensitive.

"Hi, Kimmy," he added, and gave me a heart-melting smile as he walked by.

I blushed and stammered something unintelligible, then pushed my glasses up my nose.

"Oh, very smooth," Jane told me.

I sighed. How could I possibly be so hopeless? I had to change. I just had to! But where could I begin?

Books by Cherie Bennett

Wild Hearts
Wild Hearts on Fire

Available from ARCHWAY Paperbacks

WILD HEARTS on Fire

CHERIE BENNETT

AN ARCHWAY PAPERBACK
Published by POCKET BOOKS

New York   London   Toronto   Sydney   Tokyo   Singapore

This book is a work of fiction. Names, characters, places, and incidents either are products of the author's imagination or are used fictitiously. Any resemblance to actual events or locales or persons, living or dead, is entirely coincidental.

AN ARCHWAY PAPERBACK *ORIGINAL*

 An Archway Paperback published by
POCKET BOOKS, a division of Simon & Schuster Inc.
1230 Avenue of the Americas, New York, NY 10020

ISBN: 0-671-86514-5

First Archway Paperback printing April 1994

10 9 8 7 6 5 4 3 2 1

AN ARCHWAY PAPERBACK and colophon are registered trademarks of Simon & Schuster Inc.

Cover photos by Michel Le Grou/Media Photo Group

Printed in the U.S.A.

IL: 7+

For my incredibly cool nieces and nephews:

April, Chad, Shannon, Juliet, Maia, Serena, David, and the latest arrival, Matthew—congrats, Jamie and David!

CHAPTER 1

"Sawyer Paxton doesn't even know I'm alive."

That's what I told Savy Leeman in her basement music room that Saturday morning. Savy, who has been my best friend forever, started teasing me about what a cute couple Sawyer and I would make. She knows I have the hugest crush on Sawyer, and she also knows I can barely breathe in his presence, much less open my mouth to carry on an actual conversation. But, see, Savy is a terrible tease. Everyone in her whole huge, strange, and wonderful family is a terrible tease, and since they are all my favorite people in the world, I've had to learn to put up with it.

It is, after all, much more fun hanging out at Savy's chaotic house than at my own. Not that I'm entirely sure which house *is* my own, really. My parents—both richer than sin—are divorced, and they have joint custody of me. I have a room in Mom's mansion in Belle Meade, this very rich section of Nashville, and another room in Dad's mansion in Green Hills, this other very rich section of Nashville. I have an older brother, Jason, but he's away at college. My parents are both busy all the time. My dad is first violinist for the symphony, and my mom runs the Carrier Foundation, our family's charity trust. Most of the time I think they don't even know which house I'm in on which nights. That is, unless they're fighting and I become the pawn. Then suddenly they both want me "home" with them. Savy's house is always a mess, but it feels more like home than either of my parents' houses.

"He does too know you're alive, Kimmy," Savy insisted. "He invited you to play on his demo, didn't he?"

This was true. Sawyer Paxton is the son of Judd Paxton, this really famous country songwriter, and Sawyer is incredibly talented, too. After he heard me play lead guitar with the pit band for the school musical, he actually asked me if I'd be interested in playing on his new demo. In case you don't know, that means a demonstration tape of a new song. People make demos all the time in Nashville, which is the songwriting center of the entire universe. When Sawyer asked me to play on his demo, I thought I'd died and gone to heaven.

Sawyer wasn't the only one who was surprised when I played lead guitar in the pit band during Green Hills High's production of *Grease*. No one at school even knew I played guitar, much less that I played well, except Savy.

The reason is ... well, I'm shy. Really shy. I mean really, *really* shy.

People act as if being shy is some kind of big crime or something. Well, I didn't ask to be shy. It's just the way I am. I watch Savy, who is Miss Congeniality but in a good way, and I marvel that being outgoing comes so naturally to her. I've spent most of my life wishing I could blend into the woodwork. No one expects anything of you if you blend into the woodwork.

The way I see it is, if no one expects anything of you, then no one can be disappointed.

My parents once forced me to go to a therapist. I was having bad nightmares, and my mother was weirded out over the fact that I had a tendency to daydream and just space out for a while. This therapist said I was afraid to try to live up to my parents' expectations. I suppose that's true. Everyone in my family has been so . . . awesome. You know, judges, senators, famous composers, things like that.

I never wanted to be a judge or a senator or a famous composer. I would settle for going out on an actual date before I graduate from high school.

It's not that I'm horrid-looking. I'm tall, though—five feet nine. I hate being tall because everyone stares at you if you're tall. I'm skinny, too. Savy says models are tall and skinny and I should thank the good Lord nightly for my excellent genes, but she only says this because she is short with a tendency to be plump. Did you ever notice how people always seem to want what they can't have in this world? I have long blond hair and blue eyes. The blue eyes part is kind of nice, I guess, but since I'm as blind as a bat without my glasses no one ever actually sees my eyes to appreciate their color. I've tried wearing contact lenses, but they irritate my eyes so much that I can't stand them.

Savy rags on me all the time because I wear baggy clothes and she says I slouch, which I suppose I do, but you'd slouch and wear baggy clothes, too, if you were tall and skinny and had a major bosom. Talk about embarrassing.

Still, I don't think I'm so horrid that no one

would ever ask me out. Well, actually I *have* been asked out. I've just never been asked out by anyone I'd ever want to go out *with*.

"Here's how to get Sawyer," Savy said, pulling me out of my reverie. "Just go right up to him at school, grab him by the shirt, and plant a big ole kiss on him."

I gave her a look. "Before American history class or after?" I asked dryly.

"Oh, during, maybe," Savy mused, winding one red curl around her finger. "Speaking for myself, I'm getting sick of hearing about the Civil War. A kiss would really liven things up."

"It's called the War Between the States," I reminded her, reaching for my guitar and looping the strap around my neck. "Anyone would think you were a Yankee, calling it the Civil War."

"Speaking of Yankees, here I am," Jane McVay announced, coming into Savy's huge basement music room. "And may I remind you which side won the war?"

"Well, don't let the news get around," Savy teased. "A lot of southerners haven't been informed."

"Yeah, tell me about it," Jane agreed. "I think the pastel people would curl up and die."

I watched with admiration as Jane strode over to the set of drums. She is like no one else

I've ever met in my life. She recently moved to Nashville from New York City, when her dad got transferred. She is an incredibly great drummer—in New York she went to that famous school, the High School of Performing Arts—and by far the coolest girl I ever met.

She's funny, too. For example, she calls the rich, snobby kids at Green Hills High—the ones who think they run the school and hence everyone's life—"the pastel people," in honor of the flowery pastel outfits the girls wear.

The pastel people make fun of Jane all the time. Frankly, I would just die if they snickered at me the way they snicker at Jane. Basically she's normal-looking—brown hair, brown eyes, average height and weight. Except for the six earrings she wears in one ear, she could pretty much blend into a crowd if she wanted to. She doesn't want to. Jane dresses—how can I put it?—uniquely. Every day she wears a different costume to school. She is her own personal art project. At band practice she dresses normally—like today she had on jeans and an Elvis T-shirt—but at school she might dress like a Girl Scout one day and a nun the next.

"Where's Sandra?" Jane asked, getting settled behind the drums.

Sandra Farrell is the fourth member of our band, Wild Hearts.

Oh, that's right, I didn't tell you about the band yet.

It's only the most exciting thing that's ever happened to me in my entire life.

Here's how it happened. Savy was the musical director for our school play. She was set to play keyboards, Jane agreed to be the drummer, and Sandra Farrell, who is smart, cool, and number one in our class, agreed to play bass. Savy begged me to play guitar in the pit band, but I turned her down. I mean, I had never, ever, *ever* played in front of anyone but her. I would just spend hours practicing by myself in my room at my mother's house or at my father's house, staring into the mirror and pretending I was some hot babe from MTV. The idea of playing in front of our entire school was the scariest thing I could think of. No, I just couldn't do it.

So Savy asked Wyatt Shane, this guy in our class who has his own rock band, Thunder Rolls. Now, I admit, Wyatt is extremely cute, but he is also totally stuck on himself and a complete jerk. Also, I believed in my heart of hearts that I was a better guitar player.

Well, one night Jane went out with Wyatt, and Wyatt stole Jane's mom's car. It's a really long story, but in short, he'd been drinking and he got into a car accident and broke his arm the day before dress rehearsal for the play. Savy, Jane, and Sandra pleaded with me to replace him. Savy said I was the only guitarist in school good enough to jump in at the last minute. And . . . I finally said yes.

So we played together. And the only way I can describe it is, it was magic. Playing with Savy, Jane, and Sandra was the most fun I ever had in my life.

Then Savy got this bright idea that we should form our own band. She's the most persuasive person I know, and she talked all of us into agreeing with her. We came up with the name Wild Hearts—pretty terrif, don't you think?

That was just a week ago, and though we hadn't played in public yet, we'd already had three practices. And even though Savy wants us to be a country band and Wyatt's band plays heavy metal rock, I think we already sound better than Thunder Rolls.

"Sandra called and said she'd be a few minutes late," Savy said, doodling a melody on the piano. "She had to fill in at the gym and teach an extra aerobics class this morning."

"Well, I have to split by one o'clock," Jane reminded us, fiddling with one of her earrings. "I have to be at work by one-thirty."

After Wyatt wrecked Jane's mom's car, the

insurance had gone up by a thousand dollars. Mrs McVay had told Jane she had to get an after-school job to pay for the extra cost. She'd started the night before at Uncle Zap's, a music store at the Green Hills Mall.

"How's the job?" Savy asked Jane.

Jane rolled her eyes. "Well, I sit behind this counter and watch my IQ slump. Then someone comes over with a CD and I ring it up, take the money, put the CD in a bag, and repeat. Over and over and over."

"At least your parents let you play in the band," I said softly.

"Yeah, I was supposed to be grounded for, like, the rest of my life," Jane said. "But I gave them this rap about how miserable I was here, being new and all, and how music was the only thing that was keeping me from committing suicide." She shrugged and reached for the drumsticks. "You know, your basic guilt-jerk."

"Hi, sorry I'm late," Sandra said, bustling into the room. "I ran into Timmy upstairs," she added, throwing her purse on the overstuffed couch. "He said to tell Jane hello, and then he made kissing noises and cow eyes."

Timmy is Savy's little brother. He's six, and is sometimes stuck in a wheelchair because he has juvenile rheumatoid arthritis. Timmy is darling, and he has a huge crush on Jane.

"I love him, too," Jane said with a chuckle.

Savy looked Sandra over in her high-cut red leotard and black and red Lycra tights covered by cutoff jeans. "You are in the best shape of anybody I know," she told Sandra with an envious sigh.

"If you taught aerobics and were captain of the tennis team, you'd be in good shape, too," I pointed out to Savy.

"No, I probably wouldn't," Savy replied, lifting her curls off her neck. "I'd probably still be pudgy. I have pudgy genes."

"If you were on a disciplined workout program, you could change that," Sandra told Savy, taking her bass guitar out of its case.

Sandra is the most disciplined girl I've ever met. In addition to teaching aerobics, being captain of the tennis team, and number one academically, she is president of the junior class, plays four musical instruments, and does charity work for the homeless. Sandra is one of the few black kids at Green Hills High, but she hangs out with everybody. Some kids resent her for this, which I think is just ridiculous. She's cute and smart and incredibly accomplished. Actually, a lot of people are kind of intimidated by her.

Actually, I am one of those people.

I mean, Sandra is always so confident about

everything. When I'm around her, I feel even wussier than usual.

I pushed my glasses farther up my nose while Sandra tuned her bass.

"Ready when you are," she said, tightening her G-string.

"Okay, let's warm up with 'Boot Scootin' Boogie,'" Savy suggested. She adjusted her vocal mike at the piano so that it perfectly faced her mouth. "Y'all want to test your mikes?"

"Testing, testing," we all called into our mikes.

"Hey, check, paycheck," Jane called into the mike set up by her drums.

"Let's do it," Sandra said.

Savy counted us off, and we launched into the tune. It was a fun up-tempo country song by Brooks and Dunn. Savy sang lead, per usual—Savy has a great voice—and the rest of us came in on harmony parts on the chorus. During the instrumental parts we each took a solo. Then we came back in on the chorus and brought the song home.

"Who's singing the fifth?" Sandra asked when we finished the song. She meant who was supposed to be singing the notes five steps above the melody.

"Me," I admitted, my face burning red. Had I been flat and not even realized it?

"Turn Kimmy's mike down a little, Savy," Sandra suggested. "Her voice is so strong that it's competing too much with the melody."

"Mine?" I squeaked. I barely considered myself capable of carrying a tune.

"Don't you know you have a great voice?" Jane asked me.

"No," I replied, pushing some hair behind my ear, "because I don't. Savy has the great voice. I'm not even in choir!"

"You do have a great voice," Savy agreed. She turned my mike down a little.

"I don't think so," I mumbled. "I must have just been screaming too loud by mistake." I tuned my guitar nervously.

"How is it that you manage to turn every compliment into an insult?" Sandra asked, looking bemused.

"I don't," I protested. "I mean, I'm not . . . Well, sorry," I finally managed, blushing furiously.

"Let's try 'It Wasn't God Who Made Honky Tonk Angels,'" Savy said, graciously changing the subject.

"Oh, gawd, gag me with a spoon, Kitty Wells, it's so country!" Jane groaned. Jane

12

hates most country music, so this is always an uphill battle for Savy.

"Yeah, but our arrangement is completely new and hip, very rock 'n' roll!" Savy pointed out.

"And the harmonies are great," Sandra added, "if I do say so myself." Sandra had written the harmony parts for us.

"Yeah, okay," Jane agreed reluctantly, "but after this one, how about if we really rock out? If I play much more of this I'm gonna want to go home and watch 'Hee Haw' or something." Jane shuddered at the notion.

We launched into our version of the old Kitty Wells tune, and we really sounded great. We did it a lot faster than the original, and I got a chance to add some really cool guitar licks. When we finished, someone applauded from the doorway.

"Yes, ma'am, you girls sound mighty fine!" an older woman whooped.

It was Savy's grandmother, whom we all called Gramma Beth. Gramma Beth has fiery red hair and dresses like a gypsy. She's also the best fiddle player I've ever heard.

"Thanks," Savy replied with a huge grin. "We're really making progress, don't you think?"

"Lawd, yes," Gramma Beth agreed. She

moved briskly into the room, her dozens of bangle bracelets tinkling musically on her arms. "I think ya'll are ready to show the world what you can do."

"Oh, no, we're not!" I insisted quickly, appalled at the very thought. Everyone turned to look at me. "Well, I mean, we need a lot more practice," I added meekly.

"Oh, shoot, child, you'd hide your light under a bushel basket forever if we didn't push you now and then," Gramma Beth drawled. "Now, here's what I suggest. A week from next Friday night there's a big to-do fundraiser for the Juvenile Arthritis Foundation out to the Opryland Hotel. I'm co-chairwoman, and I bet you I could get you girls on the bill with Wynonna. What do you think?"

Savy's face lit up. "You mean Wynonna Judd? *The* Wynonna Judd?"

"I sure do," Gramma Beth said. "What if ya'll did, oh, let's say three tunes. How would that be?"

"Cool," Jane pronounced.

"Fabulous!" Savy cried.

"Fine," Sandra agreed.

"Horrible!" I screamed.

They all turned to look at me again.

"We're not ready!" I insisted.

"So we'll get ready," Savy said. "We have almost two weeks to practice three tunes."

"But ... but ..." I sputtered.

"Did you think we were going to play in Savy's basement forever?" Sandra asked archly.

"No, of course not," I replied with dignity, even though at that moment I wanted nothing more than to be assured that I would never, ever actually have to play in public.

"Kimmy, you sound so hot," Jane told me. "I am, like, the world's toughest music critic, you know."

I wiped my damp palms on the legs of my baggy jeans. "I think we should have a date planned ... say, two months or so from now," I said hesitantly.

"So you can have two months to freak out," Sandra stated. "And in two months you'll want two more months."

"I just want us to be the best," I mumbled, since I knew Sandra was probably right.

"Well, I say we vote," Savy suggested. "All those in favor of having Wild Hearts make their debut at the Opryland fund-raiser a week from Friday, raise your hand."

Every hand went up but mine, including Gramma Beth's.

"You lose," Jane sang out, as if that wasn't obvious.

"Wait. Maybe this should be unanimous," Savy said kindly. "I don't want Kimmy to be forced into something she doesn't want to do."

I gave her a grateful smile.

Savy got up from the piano and came over to me. "Remember when you thought you would absolutely die if you played in front of everyone at school, and then it turned out to be the best thing you ever did?" she asked me.

I nodded mutely.

"This is like that, only better," Savy said earnestly. "You are really great, Kimmy, really talented. You have to look at this like . . . like it's your destiny. And I promise we'll make sure the band is ready. What do you say?"

I looked at all of their serious faces as they waited to hear what I'd say. Suddenly an image flashed into my mind: me, onstage in front of hundreds of screaming fans. I'm wearing an awesome-looking red bra top and jeans and cowboy boots. My hair is real wild-looking, my blue eyes sparkle with confidence, and I am playing the guitar better than Jimi Hendrix. I finish the number, the fans go wild, I run off-stage, and there is Sawyer Paxton. He tells me I'm the hottest guitar player he's ever heard in his life and he's crazy about me. He takes me in his arms and—

"Earth to Kimmy. Are you still with us?" Savy called to me.

It wasn't impossible, was it? I mean, maybe if Sawyer heard me play with Wild Hearts he'd do more than just ask me to play on his demo. Maybe he'd actually ask me out on an actual date.

My heart was thudding in my chest. If I said yes, it could be the beginning of a new, confident, sexy me. If I said no, I could remain boyfriend-free for the rest of my life. On the other hand, no was safe. I was used to saying no.

I made a decision and took a deep breath.

"Yes," I finally uttered.

"Yeah, Kimmy!" Savy squeaked. Everyone applauded, and Savy hugged me hard.

There was no way I could back out now.

Wild Hearts was about to be turned loose on the world.

CHAPTER
2
❤

*B*uz-z-z-z-z-z-z.

I reached over and pushed the button on my alarm clock and closed my eyes again. It was Monday morning. The start of another school week. Actually, I like school—that is to say, I like learning, which occasionally happens inside of our high school, but in my opinion not nearly as often as it should. I'm a very good student—I work hard at it—and I plan to get into a good college. I'm hoping college will involve people who are excited about learning, unlike high school, where people are more excited about who has recently broken up with whom.

Or maybe it's just because I am such a social zero that I take this attitude.

I showered and washed my hair and dressed in tan cotton pants and a baggy white cotton sweater. Once my hair was dry I brushed it and stuck it back in a low ponytail with one of those covered elastic things. Then I put on my glasses, picked up my books and my purse, and headed down to breakfast.

"Oh, hello, dear," my mother said from her place at the long, long dining room table. She sounded surprised to see me. Obviously she hadn't realized that I'd spent the night at her house. I didn't think of either my father's or my mother's house as "my" house, since they'd both moved after their divorce, so I hadn't lived in either house as part of an actual family.

"Good morning," I said, sitting down near her.

She rang a little bell, and Mrs. Gruller came out of the kitchen.

"Mornin', sweetie," Mrs. Gruller said. She is a nice woman—middle-aged, tall, and thin with crinkly laugh lines around her eyes. She's my mother's assistant. She does a little of everything, including cooking meals on the rare occasions when my mother is actually home to eat. Her husband is Mom's chauffeur, handyman, and security person. The Grullers live in a cute cottage on the back part of our property.

"What would you like for breakfast?"

"Juice and cereal, please," I told her. Of course I was capable of getting my own juice and cereal, but that is not the way things are done at Mother's.

"You got it," Mrs. Gruller said cheerfully. She put a bone china teacup and saucer in front of me and patted my head kindly, then went back into the kitchen.

"So . . ." my mother said, folding her hands in that proper way she has. My mother is a patrician-looking beauty who wears her blond hair in a perfect bun at the back of her perfect head. Even at seven-thirty in the morning she was well groomed. "I didn't even know you were here."

"So I gathered," I told her, pouring myself some tea from the tea set on the table.

"I didn't hear you come in," my mother said, sipping her tea daintily.

"It was pretty late, after band practice," I added pointedly. My mother has offered me every bribe in the world to get me to play something other than rock and country. Professional classical musicians abound in our family on both sides, and she cringes whenever she hears me playing the guitar in my room.

Also, she doesn't think I have any talent.

"We named the band. Did I tell you that?" I continued, ignoring the obvious—she did not want to hear about it. "We're calling ourselves Wild Hearts."

Mrs. Gruller came in and set a glass of fresh-squeezed orange juice and a bowl of cereal in front of me. I put my napkin on my lap.

Mother sighed. "Is this supposed to be your way of sticking my nose in it? Going on about it like this?"

"Going on about it like what?" I asked innocently. "You're my mother. You're supposed to be interested in my activities."

"I *am* interested in your activities," my mother said, patting her mouth with her napkin. "I just wish you'd choose more appropriate activities with more appropriate company."

This was a dig about Savy. Not only is Savy's family kind of bohemian, but Savy and her family are Jewish. Now, my parents are supposed to be these big liberals, which is why they send me to public school, but in her heart of hearts I believe my mother is a snob. A racist, anti-Semitic snob.

Imagine when I told her our bass player was black.

"And another thing," my mother continued.

"I've told you time and again that if you'll let me know where you are, I'll have Mr. Gruller pick you up."

"I don't want Mr. Gruller to pick me up from band practice," I said in a low, intense voice. "It's bad enough I have to have him drive me to and from school."

"You know why that's necessary," my mother said evenly. "It's not some capricious notion, Kimberly."

Yes, I knew why. I'd only had nightmares about it my entire life.

Years ago my brother, Jason, was kidnapped and held for ransom because my family is so rich. Jason was only six years old, and the kidnappers buried him alive out on some deserted farm near Smyrna, in a box with a tiny airhole. He was in that box for four days before the police were able to trap the kidnappers and find my brother. He was only half conscious from lack of oxygen. He almost died.

I was just a baby then, since Jason is five years older than me. But because of what happened with him my parents have been overprotective of me my entire life. I know that sounds kind of strange since, as I said, they don't usually know which house I'm in. Look, I never said they were consistent. They make me wear a beeper so that they can buzz me at any time of the day or night. And since Jason got kid-napped coming out of school, they insist that the chauffeur drive me to and from school every day. If I'm going with friends, Mr. Gruller just watches to see that I get into the friends' car. He does this from afar. I don't think any kids at school realize this, except for Savy. I would die of embarrassment if they all knew.

"Ya'll need anything else?" Mrs. Gruller asked, coming back into the dining room.

"I don't think so," my mother replied. "If you could just ring Mr. Gruller and tell him Kimmy needs a ride to school ..."

"Sure," Mrs. Gruller agreed, and she disap-peared into the kitchen.

"If I had my own car I could drive myself to school." I'd said this to my mother a hun-dred times before, but I just couldn't seem to give up.

"We've been over this ground," my mother said with a sigh.

"But I've got the beeper!" I exclaimed. "I could always beep you if anything happened. Besides, you don't know where I am half the time. The whole thing just isn't logical!"

"Kimberly, this is one of the few things that your father and I agree on," my mother said.

"So I don't think you're going to make any headway."

"What happens when I go to college?" I pressed, getting up from the dining room table. "Are you going to send me there with bodyguards?"

"If I have to," my mother said evenly.

"Fine, make my life miserable," I snapped, picking up my books and my purse from the sideboard.

"If your life is miserable, Kimberly," my mother said in that irritatingly all-knowing voice, "it is no one's responsibility but your own."

I stomped out to the Rolls and got in the back, slamming the door hard before Mr. Gruller could do it for me. I absolutely, positively could not talk to my mother.

She didn't understand anything at all, and she never would.

"Hi, Kimmy," Dave Mallone said eagerly as I slid into my seat next to him in my first period class, English.

"Hi," I replied, smiling at him. The reason that I can smile at Dave Mallone is he is even shyer than I am. Seriously. He can't even speak up in class, even though he's really smart. He has pale, sort of see-through skin, pale hair, and pale eyelashes. The same kids who make fun of Jane make fun of Dave, but for different reasons. I was always nice to Dave. For one thing, I have a fondness for underdogs. And for another thing, I hate cruelty of any kind. The pastel people were cruel to Dave. They called him Weenie Mallone, or the Invisible Man on account of his being so pale and never opening his mouth.

Dave and I had gone to school together for years. He was the first guy who ever asked me out on a date, in eighth grade. He invited me to our middle school's carnival. I turned him down by making an excuse about how I had something else I had to do, which wasn't true. All it meant was that in an effort to not hurt his feelings I couldn't go to the carnival with Savy. Actually, he was also the last person who had asked me out. At the end of the tenth grade, he'd invited me to the tenth grade dance. That time I said I'd be out of town with my mother.

"Did you write the paper on Tennessee Williams?" he asked me, blinking his pale eyelashes rapidly.

"Yep," I replied, pulling my paper out of my notebook. Our English teacher, Ms. Cavelli, had assigned a paper on the American playwright of our choice.

"So . . . how's your band going?" he asked me, biting nervously at his lower lip.

"Oh, fine," I said. I didn't want to talk about Wild Hearts, unless it was to get my mother's goat. Talking about the band reminded me that we were going to be performing in public a week from Friday. Oh, God.

Dave attempted what passed as a smile. "Did I tell you how good you were when you played for the school play?" he asked me.

"You know you did," I reminded him gently.

"Yeah," he agreed, and bit at a hangnail on his pinky. "Well, I wanted to tell you again."

"Thanks, Dave," I said.

Ms. Cavelli strode into the room, so that was the end of my painful conversation with Dave.

Poor guy. If I was a social zero, he was a social subatomic particle.

When class ended I hurried into the hall where I usually met Savy, and then we walked to biology together. By the time I met her at our usual corner she was standing there with Sandra and Jane. I noticed right away how cute they all looked. Savy had on hot pink baggy jeans and a short crocheted sweater, Sandra wore khaki shorts and a green and white striped shirt, and Jane was dressed in a

Girl Scout uniform, with a necklace of plastic Girl Scout cookies hanging around her neck.

"I'm not kidding," Sandra was saying, holding out a piece of paper. "It's going to be an amazing class."

"Hi, what's up?" I asked them.

"Wonder Woman here is trying to persuade us to take this new self-defense seminar for women at her gym," Jane reported, pointing to the flyer in Sandra's hand.

"It's supposed to be a really great seminar," Sandra told us. "Don't you guys want to feel like you can defend yourselves?" Sandra says 'you guys' instead of 'ya'll' because she lived in Detroit before she moved to Nashville. It's these little things that brand someone a Yankee right away.

"No," Savy replied. "I want Billy Dean to defend me." Billy Dean is an extremely cute up-and-coming country star.

Sandra gave Savy a look of disgust. "Is Billy planning to follow the band around? Because he might want to be thinking about his own career."

"How shallow of him," Savy scoffed.

"Listen, I'm serious," Sandra continued. "Wild Hearts is going to be incredibly successful, which means crowds of people, crazed fans, guys on the loose, you know . . ."

"As Gramma Beth would say, 'From your mouth to God's ear,' " Savy put in fervently.

"I just think it would be smart if we all felt like we could take care of ourselves," Sandra said briskly. She pointed to the flyer. "What's the big deal? It's just three hours tomorrow night. Come on, we can fit that in. And you can all have my gym discount, so it'll be cheap."

"Wait. Do we, like, *sweat* in this class?" Jane asked.

"No, nubile boys fan you as you throw spit-wads at the bad guys," Sandra said sarcastically.

"The only place I sweat is onstage behind the drums," Jane said. "Or in bed with Christian Slater," she added.

"Well, I'm taking it," Sandra said. "I think you guys should plan ahead on this. It would be a really smart thing to do."

"Hi," Sawyer Paxton said as he walked past us in the hall. My heart beat in double time just to look at him. How could any one human guy be so incredible-looking? He had on jeans and a red rugby shirt with a blue logo that matched the blue of his eyes. And it wasn't just that he was so cute. He was smart, too. And talented. And sensitive.

"Hi, Kimmy," he added, and gave me a heart-melting smile as he walked by.

I blushed and stammered something unintelligible, then pushed my glasses up my nose.

"Oh, very smooth," Jane told me.

I sighed. How could I possibly be so hopeless? I had to change. I just had to! But where could I begin?

A self-defense class! Yes! That really would be a beginning. And maybe if I really did learn self-defense, my mother would be so impressed that she'd let me get my own car. There I'd be, dressed in something tiny and sexy, sitting behind the wheel of my convertible. Sawyer would be beside me, a tape of *Wild Hearts' Greatest Hits* blasting from the incredible sound system. He would reach over to play with my hair, then he'd whisper in my ear how sexy it was that I was so strong, and then he'd—

"Kimmy, are you with us?" Savy asked.

"What? Oh, sure," I said, pushing some hair back that had slipped from my ponytail.

"Well, I'm doing this," Sandra said, shoving the flyer back into her notebook. "You guys are missing out on something good."

"I'm doing it, too," I piped up.

"You?" Jane asked.

I nodded. "I think it sounds like ... uh ... fun."

"Fun?" Jane repeated, as if I'd lost my mind.

"Cool, Kimmy!" Savy cried, enthusiastic as always. "I think so, too, actually."

"Well, your opinion doesn't count," Jane said. "You're up for everything."

"Not math," Savy pointed out.

"So come on, McVay, don't be the only holdout!" Sandra said. "Besides, a tough New York girl like you ought to be great at a butt-kicking class."

"Gee, much as I'd love to be a part of your happy group, I have to work at Uncle Zap's tomorrow night. Sorry!" Jane said, popping some gum into her mouth.

Sandra shrugged. "Too bad." She turned to me and Savy. "Wear baggy clothes you can move in."

"I always wear baggy clothes," I pointed out ruefully.

"That's true, you do," Sandra realized. "Well, then, you're all set."

"Just remember, we have band practice right after school," Savy said. "We have to decide which three tunes we're doing for the Opry-land show."

The Opryland show. Playing in public. Oh, God.

I closed my eyes. "Maybe I'll get sick," I thought hopefully.

"If you get sick, we'll kill you," Sandra told me cheerfully. "Later!" She hurried off to class, and Jane, Savy, and I scurried toward the biology lab.

Just as I was rounding the corner I saw Sawyer again, and I tripped over absolutely nothing and almost fell. I looked behind me at the floor, the way people always do when they trip, and then I stumbled into the lab.

Maybe I should have thought about learning to walk before I contemplated self-defense.

CHAPTER

3

☙

"Okay, ladies, find seats on the floor, please," the instructor called to us.

It was the next night. A dozen women of various ages, sizes, shapes, and colors were mingling at the Work House, the gym where Sandra taught aerobics.

I sat down with Savy and Sandra and nervously eyed the instructor. She was somewhere in her thirties or forties, I would guess, and in perfect physical shape. She work a white T-shirt and baggy fatigue pants. Her brown hair was up in a ponytail, and muscles rippled in her upper arms.

"I'm Nancy Larsen," she told us. "Welcome to Self-Defense for Women. I hope that after tonight you will be a different woman than you are now—less fearful, stronger, braver, and smarter. How does that sound?"

A murmur of approval went around the room.

"Easy for her to say," I whispered to Savy. "Her forearms are bigger than my waist."

"Shhhh," Savy whispered back.

"Now, no one is going to leave here a black belt in karate—although some of you might decide to look into that after this mini-class," Nancy said, pacing across the front of the gym. "What we want to get from this session is street smarts. First, we want to get over the idea that, because you are female and probably smaller and not as physically strong as men, you cannot defend yourselves against the scum element. Because you can."

"How about against blind dates?" one girl called out. Some others giggled.

"Actually, she has a good point," Nancy said. "Date rape is by far the most common form of rape. Okay, let's all stand up and begin by exercising our vocal chords."

"Singing lessons?" I whispered to Sandra.

She gave me a look and turned her attention back to Nancy.

"First, let's all say no together," Nancy instructed.

"No," we all said.

"Well, that wouldn't discourage a flea," Nancy barked. "Now let's say it and mean it. Like this: *No!*" she yelled in a low, guttural voice.

"*No!*" we all dutifully yelled.

I felt like a total idiot.

"Good," Nancy said approvingly. "Now let's remember that men are vulnerable. They are vulnerable here"—she pointed to here eyes—"here"—she pointed to where her Adam's apple would have been if she were a man—"there"—she touched between her legs—"and here"—she indicated her instep.

"When you want to protect yourself, the first thing you do is forget about being a nice girl. Forget about being polite. When you can defend yourself, you do. When you can't, you run. The point is, you have a brain, you have resources, and you have options."

Sandra nodded solemnly, and even Savy look intrigued. Not me. I figured I would never have the nerve to yell no in a voice that sounded like a football player hurling his lunch, and then go for some guy's eye sockets. Yuck.

Nancy spent the next two hours showing us how to go for the eyes—a delightful gouging motion—and various other sensitive spots. We all had to practice on a stuffed dummy of an ugly, drooling guy and then, more carefully, on each other.

The last move she showed us was the kick to the groin, which Nancy combined into a double whammy with either the tasteful eye gouge, the Adam's apple chop, or the always popular instep stomp. I admit, I had gotten kind of bored and so I was lost in one of my daydreams. This time Sawyer and I were on a deserted island. So when it came time for me to demonstrate my skill on the dummy, I pretended he was some thug menacing this island I was on with Sawyer. "*No!*" I grunted, and stomped brutally on the dummy's instep. Then I sent my heel flying home between the legs of the dummy. The dummy, whom we had named Disgusting Dennis, went flying across the room.

"Wow!" someone cried, and then the whole class burst into applause.

I looked at Disgusting Dennis, who was lying in a heap in the corner. Had I really done that?

"Excellent!" Nancy hugged my shoulders, then turned to the class. "And that, ladies, is how it's done!"

Nancy wound up the workshop, telling us that she hoped we'd all consider taking a more in-depth class she would be teaching soon, and then the group broke up.

"Well, well, well," Sandra said as the three of us walked out to her Jeep. "I didn't know you had it in you, Kimmy."

"Neither did I," I replied honestly. "I think I just got lucky."

"It's those long legs of yours," Savy said. "My legs are so short I could barely reach Disgusting Dennis's crotch. I guess if I ever get attacked I better hope it's by a short guy!"

"Three country tunes is absolutely out," Jane stated flatly. "And we should do originals. Anyone can do cover tunes."

"But no one gets over with all originals!" Savy exclaimed.

"Savy's right," Sandra said. "Be practical. Once we get attention, we can try originals. If we do it now we'll kill this band before we even get started."

Jane made a noise of disgust. "Have you ever done anything in your life that wasn't practical?" she asked Sandra.

"Yeah, agreeing to be in this band," Sandra said coolly.

I sighed and closed my eyes. The band was getting testy. It was Friday night, and we'd been practicing all week whenever we got the chance. The trouble was, between Jane's job at Uncle Zap's, Savy's commitment to the

Greenpeace Club and all her other clubs, and Sandra's student council stuff and tennis practice and matches, we just couldn't work as much as we wanted to.

And now we only had a week until our debut. In public. Oh, God.

"Kimmy, don't zone out now," Savy called to me.

I opened my eyes quickly. "I'm not," I said. "I just hate when ya'll fight."

"Oh, this isn't fighting," Jane said cheerfully, pushing the brim of her New York Mets baseball cap farther back on her head. "Fighting is when I pulverize my little sister, Jill. You can hear her all through the cardboard walls of our apartment complex."

"How about if we vote on which songs we should do next Friday?" Savy asked, always one for finding a solution. She picked up a piece of paper from her piano. "We've got a dozen songs here on our A-list, meaning we've really spent time working on them. Three of them are originals by Jane."

"Thank you very much," Jane said, bowing over her drums.

"Five of them are new country," Savy continued, and two are country or rock classics, depending on how you look at it, and two are rock classics."

"How about one of each?" I suggested timidly.

"She just read off four categories," Sandra told me.

I blushed. I often felt as if I was trying Sandra's patience, which I probably was. Once when I said something really lame, she said to me: 'Kimmy, I do not suffer fools gladly.' I was too embarrassed to point out that my grade point was almost as high as hers and that I was not a fool.

"I know that," I replied with as much dignity as possible. "Anyway, I definitely think we should do one of Jane's original songs," I added.

"Yeah, Kimmy!" Jane cheered, giving me the thumbs-up sign.

"All in favor of doing one of Jane's songs?" Savy asked.

Jane's hand flew into the air, as did mine. Savy's hand went up; then finally Sandra's did, too.

"Why, thank you," Jane said to Sandra, a big grin on her face.

"They're good tunes, especially 'Love Won't Wait,' " Sandra said grudgingly.

"Yeah, I love that," I agreed.

"Great, now we're getting somewhere!" Savy cried. "We're doing 'Love Won't Wait.' "

"And?" Jane asked hopefully.

"Let's limit ourselves to one original for now, okay?" Sandra suggested.

"Why? So we can do 'It Wasn't God Who Made Honky Tonk Angels'?" Jane asked with disgust.

"I love that song!" I exclaimed.

"And we've really made it our own," Savy pointed out. "Anyway, it's cool. Very retro, you know?"

Jane looked over at Sandra, hoping for a vote on her side.

"Sorry," Sandra said with a shrug. "I like it, too."

"That's two down!" Savy sang out eagerly. "What's our last pick?"

"Something up-tempo?" I suggested.

Sandra nodded. "Something so that we get off really big."

" 'Great Balls of Fire'!" Savy said. "It's perfect, and we do it great."

"Classic rock," Jane agreed, nodding.

"Classic country!" Savy insisted.

She and Jane always had this argument.

"Okay, so we open with country, go to original, and then get off big, right?" Sandra summed up, plucking idly at a string on her bass.

There were nods of agreement all around.

"So, let's practice our set!" Savy said eagerly.

We ran through the three songs, and we really sounded great. Savy still needed some work on the lead vocal of the song Jane wrote, and we missed a couple of harmony lines on "It Wasn't God Who Made Honky Tonk Angels." We cooked on "Great Balls of Fire," though, and finished big.

"Food break!" Gramma Beth called from the doorway. She sailed into the room, followed by Magenta Sue, a struggling young singer-songwriter who worked part-time for the Leeman family. They carried in trays of homemade kichel, a European Jewish dessert made with sugar and nuts; pecan pie; and ambrosia, this Jell-O and marshmallow dessert found only below the Mason-Dixon line. Huge amounts of food are always served at the Leeman house. The cuisine is sort of southern Jewish, an interesting blend.

"You girls just keep sounding better and better," Gramma Beth told us as she and Magenta Sue set down the food.

"I'm hungry," came a voice from the doorway. It was Timmy in his wheelchair. He looked over at Jane and wiggled his eyebrows. "Hubba-hubba!"

Jane cracked up. "Well, come on in and eat

with me, Timmy," she told him, and he quickly wheeled himself down the ramp that ran over part of the stairs.

We all got plates and helped ourselves to dessert, and soon the entire Leeman family was down there with us, eating and talking excitedly about our upcoming debut at the Juvenile Arthritis Foundation fund-raiser.

Savy has these unbelievably cute identical twin brothers, Dustin and Dylan. They're twenty, and they both go to Vanderbilt University, a really good private university right in Nashville. When we were all little we used to play together, but once the twins got to high school and got so cute, I stopped being able to even talk to them. I bet I hadn't said more than a dozen words to them in the past four years, which is why I was so surprised when Dustin came over to me and sat right down next to me on the couch. I knew it was Dustin because he's just a tiny bit taller than Dylan, and his grin is just slightly lopsided, but in a cute way.

"Hi," he said, grinning his cute lopsided grin at me.

"Hi," I whispered, hoping I didn't have any gunk from the pecan pie stuck in my teeth. I turned away and tried to quickly scrub my front teeth with my tongue. They felt fairly gunk-free. I turned back to Dustin.

"Listen, I was watching while ya'll were playing before," he told me.

"You were?" I asked, surprised. I hadn't even noticed him, that's how into the music I'd been.

He nodded. "You are really great, Kimmy, no lie," he said.

"Oh, well, you know ..." I said lamely, shrugging my shoulders and hunching over a little more.

"No, I'm serious!" Dustin insisted. "All these years Savy kept saying how good you were, but I figured it was just best-friend talk, know what I mean?"

"Oh, uh, yeah," I agreed, pushing my glasses up my nose.

Dustin stared at my face, cocking his head to one side. "You know, I haven't seen you without those glasses for years," he realized.

"Because I can't really see without them," I replied nervously.

"Well, shoot, Kimmy, you already know what everyone here looks like, anyway." He ran his thumb over his chin contemplatively. Then he slowly reached over and took off my glasses.

I blushed the same tomato-red as the new

wallpaper half covering one wall. It seemed to me as if everyone in the room had stopped talking, as if everyone was looking at Dustin looking at my naked eyes without my glasses.

"Hey, you have great eyes," he said softly.

"They don't work great," I pointed out, staring down at my empty plate.

"I mean they're pretty, Kimmy," Dustin said. "That was a compliment."

I gulped hard and forced myself to utter a simple thank-you.

"You're welcome," Dustin said. He handed me back my glasses.

I fumbled to put them on, hating myself for acting like such an incredible dweeb in front of Dustin. Why did I act like that? I knew it wasn't who I really was, but I just couldn't seem to help myself.

We talked for a few more minutes about music, and then Savy's family left so we could practice some more. We worked on the harmony parts for "It Wasn't God Who Made Honky Tonk Angels," and Jane went over the bridge of her original for Savy.

Savy looked at her watch. "It's ten. Want to call it a night?"

"Are we going to get any time in tomorrow?" Sandra asked.

Jane shook her head no. "I have to do a

double shift at Uncle Zap's tomorrow because I took tonight off," she explained. "I can do Sunday afternoon, though."

Everyone agreed to Sunday afternoon, and we ended practice. I, for one, was always sorry when band practice ended. Everyone else seemed to have a life other than the band, but for me it was everything.

Jane walked over to me and stared at me with a funny look on her face, then she said, " 'Why, Kimmy, I've never seen you without your glasses,' " in a bass voice, imitating Dustin.

"Very funny," I replied, completely embarrassed. So I had been right. Everyone had been watching Dustin talking with me.

"My brother thinks you're as fine as the day is long," Savy drawled with a grin on her face.

"You know that isn't true, Savy," I told her.

"Well, you could be," Savy amended. "You choose not to be."

"Yeah," Sandra agreed. "You hide behind your glasses and those baggy clothes of yours."

"I wear glasses so I can see," I shot back. "And I happen to like comfortable clothes."

"God, I only wish I had your bod and face to work with," Jane said fervently, throwing herself back on the couch. She cocked her head at me. "Do you know how cute you are?"

"Yeah, right," I snorted.

"I've been telling her that for forever," Savy told Jane. "She never listens."

"You don't want to look cute, do you, Kimmy?" Sandra asked as she packed up her bass.

No one had ever put it to me exactly like that before. I really didn't know what to say. Did I want to look cute? Or did I want to just not be noticed? I mean, what if you worked at "cute" and then you failed? Wouldn't that be just awful?

"I just don't see 'cute' as being important," I said slowly. "It's not like being smart. Or nice. Or kind," I added.

"True," Jane agreed.

"First impressions count," Sandra said flatly, folding her arms. "Besides, we're in show business now, and looks definitely count in show business."

"Oh, really?" I responded defensively. "Is Elton John a beauty? Or Billy Joel?"

"I love Billy Joel," Jane said fervently.

"Exactly," I said hotly. "Ya'll just have a double standard for guys and for girls."

"The world has a double standard for guys and for girls," Sandra pointed out. "But I still don't see why you wouldn't want to look as good as you could."

"You could have your own style," Jane suggested. "No one is saying you should look like, God forbid, one of the pastel people."

"I don't have a style," I muttered.

"I have a great idea!" Savy said, jumping up from the piano bench and looking at me with excitement. "Let's find you a style!"

"Great idea!" Jane agreed. "We'll do a makeover!"

"I don't want to be made over!" I protested, folding my arms in front of me defensively. "I like me just the way I am!"

"So do we," Savy assured me.

"But wouldn't it make you feel more confident if you found your own style?" Sandra pressed. "Don't you want to stand out from the crowd?"

"No," I said honestly.

Sandra cocked her head at me. "I don't believe that. I think you really do, but you're afraid to try."

The truth of that observation really hit home. How did Sandra know that about me? I didn't say a word.

"Is Sandra right?" Savy asked me.

"I guess ... maybe ..."

"Look, Wild Hearts is definitely going to

stand out from the crowd," Jane said seriously. "You are the lead guitar player, so you better want some attention!"

"I . . . suppose," I agreed reluctantly.

"Great!" Savy cried. "How about Sunday after practice we do some major magic on Kimmy?"

"Cool," Jane agreed.

"Excellent," Sandra added.

"Good, then it's decided!" Savy exclaimed enthusiastically.

"Uh, excuse me, I didn't agree to this yet," I reminded them.

"Well?" Jane asked, her hands on her hips. "Is you in, or is you chicken?"

"Can I pick both?" I asked meekly.

"She's gonna do it!" Savy yelled happily.

"I don't want to look too wild," I cautioned them.

"Kimmy, don't you trust us?" Savy asked innocently.

"No," I said bluntly.

"Good, you shouldn't," Sandra said with a wicked grin.

"That's right," Jane agreed. "Because on Sunday you, Kimmy Carrier, will have that Alice in Wonderland experience. Yes, you are going to step through the looking glass, and a whole new Kimmy will come out the other side!"

CHAPTER
4

♋

All through band practice on Sunday I kept wondering if they remembered about this big makeover thing they'd planned. No one said a word about it. Part of me was hoping they'd forgotten about the whole idea, and part of me kind of sort of wanted to go through with it. That's me. My middle name is ambivalence.

We worked four long and hard hours, and I could hear how good we were getting. Still, the thought that we'd be appearing in public for the first time in just five days filled me with anxiety. To put it plainly, I was petrified.

Rehearsal broke up at six.

"We haven't talked unis yet," Jane said as she got up from behind the drums and stretched. "What are we going to wear Friday night?"

"We need to decide what we want our look to be," Savy mused. "What does the name Wild Hearts say?"

"It says we're independent and we don't all dress the same way," Jane said definitively. "Bands who dress alike are too lame to live."

"Yes, but we still need some kind of unifying look," Sandra said firmly.

"A certain color, maybe," Savy suggested, "but with our own style?"

"I don't have a style," I reminded her.

"Yes, but we're changing all that this afternoon," she told me with a grin.

Oh. So she *did* remember.

"Hey, I have an idea!" Savy exclaimed. "How about a different girl-type costume on each of us. You know, one cheerleader, one ballerina, one Girl Scout, one . . . I don't know, something else. It would be funny and unique and would be making fun of stereotypes!"

"You're talking about how I dress every day," Jane said. "I want people to concentrate on the music."

"Everyone hates the idea?" Savy asked us.

Sandra and I nodded.

"Okay," Savy said with an easy shrug. "It was just a thought."

"Let's go back to the idea of certain colors but our own style," Sandra suggested. "That could work. We'd each need to pick something kind of theatrical, but something that shows our own personality."

"Black?" Jane suggested.

"With something bright, though," Savy mused, "Red? Hot pink?"

"Hey, I just thought of something," Sandra said. "My mom gets all her stage costumes at Dangerous Threads. You get a great discount if you're a professional musician. How about if we all go there together and find our stage outfits?"

"I love the clothes there," Savy said wistfully. "But I am on a seriously limited budget."

"Mine's even worse," Jane added. "Until I pay my mother back the thousand bucks I owe her, I can't afford to buy a stick of gum."

"I wouldn't mind putting it on my credit card," I offered hesitantly. "I mean, ya'll could pay me back later."

"Oh, we couldn't let you do that—" Savy began.

"Yes, we could," Jane interrupted. "It's for the band, so it's cool. I'll pay you back, Kimmy. What's a few more weeks of indentured servitude at Uncle Zap's, anyway?"

"So do we all agree?" Sandra asked.

We did.

"We could go over right now," she continued, looking at her watch. "They're open until ten tonight."

"First we have to take Kimmy through the looking glass," Jane reminded everyone. "It's National Kimmy Makeover Day."

"Do we have to?" I asked meekly.

"Yes!" they all said, and they dragged me upstairs to Savy's room to do the dastardly deed.

I didn't look.

For two hours they worked on my hair and my makeup. After they'd washed my hair, they squished tons of mousse into it, then made me hang my head over the edge of Savy's bed while they blew it dry from underneath. Then they put all this makeup on my face—blush and eyeliner and mascara and lipstick. I kept protesting that I didn't want to look like a clown, and they kept telling me to hush up.

Once they were happy with my appearance from the neck up—they still wouldn't let me look in the mirror—they decided I should try on some of Savy's clothes. Keep in mind that Savy is seven inches shorter than I am and we weigh about the same. I knew a truly ridiculous notion when I heard one.

"Ya'll have really lost your minds," I told them. "Savy's clothes will never fit me."

"Well, the clothes you wear now don't fit you, either," Jane pointed out.

That was true. I always bought large or extra-large everything.

"I've got just the thing!" Savy cried, running to her closet. She took out a sheer high-waisted hot pink baby-doll dress with a scoop neck, and held it up for all of us to see.

"Not in this lifetime!" I protested. I had seen this dress on Savy. The front was low-cut and revealing.

"But it'll fit!" Savy assured me. "It's loose-fitting, and the waistline is supposed to be high. And it's really long on me, so it'll just be a mini on you!"

"I don't wear hot pink!" I cried. "I can't!"

"Just try it on," Jane coaxed me. "If you hate it, you can take it off."

"You can see through it!" I protested.

Savy rummaged in her drawer. "Here," she said, thrusting a lacy white low-cut cat suit at me. "You wear this underneath. One size fits all."

"I can't—" I began.

"You can," Sandra said.

"You will," Savy added. She handed me the dress, and I reluctantly took it. I was too shy to change in front of them, so I went into Savy's bathroom. They had covered her mirror with towels so I couldn't even see my own reflection.

I pulled off my baggy white cotton shirt and long navy skirt and stepped into the lace cat suit. The legs didn't come down to my ankles like they did on Savy, but instead ended at mid-calf. Well, I supposed that was okay. The top was dangerously skimpy. It barely covered my bra. I kept pulling at the neckline, but there wasn't much material there to pull. The cleavage that I'd spent my life camouflaging was right there for the world to gawk at.

Well, maybe the dress would cover it up.

I slipped the baby-doll dress over my head. It was cut even lower than the cat suit, so that the white lace peeked out above the neckline.

And the hem ended just south of my panties.

"Ya'll, this doesn't fit!" I called out to them.

"Let us see!" Savy begged from the other side of the door.

"But there's no point!" I yelled back. "I look like my clothes shrunk!"

"You don't know, because you can't see," Jane pointed out, "unless you cheated and took the towels off the mirror."

"I didn't," I called back.

"So come on out," Sandra directed me.

With a sigh, I reluctantly pulled open the door and walked into Savy's room.

They all looked at me with their jaws hanging open.

"Okay, I look like a total fool," I said, folding my arms self-consciously over my half-bare chest. "I told you I did."

Silence.

"Kimmy," Savy finally said, "you are gorgeous."

"I doubt it," I replied, and turned on my heel to head back into the bathroom.

"She's telling you the truth," Sandra said.

I stopped and turned back to them. "Say what?"

"You are a stone fox," Jane said with glee. "This is too cool!"

"Are ya'll making fun of me?" I asked slowly.

Savy's grin spread across her face like molasses on a hot day. She took my hand and positioned me in front of her full-length mirror. Then she stood on one side, and Jane and Sandra stood on the other, and they ceremoniously undraped the mirror, letting the towels fall to the floor.

Some other girl was standing there.

"I . . . I . . ." I stammered, staring at myself wide-eyed. My image was kind of blurry because I didn't have my glasses on, but still, really pretty is really pretty, and really pretty is what I looked.

Imagine that. I was pretty.

The makeup they'd put on me was tasteful, and my hair looked wild and sexy. The dress was too short, but because of the lacy cat suit underneath I didn't look naked. The top of the dress was low-cut, but since the rest of the dress was loose, it didn't look sleazy, just, well . . . kind of fabulous.

"Are you hot or are you hot?" Jane crowed.

"I just can't believe it," I breathed, turning this way and that in the mirror.

"We'll show you how we did your makeup and everything, so you can do it yourself," Savy said eagerly. "And we can buy you some makeup and clothes."

"I'm not sure," I said hesitantly, but I was still admiring my image in the mirror.

"You'll never be sure," Sandra said. "But it's like my mom says. You have to act *as if.* In other words, if you act *as if* you feel confident, eventually confidence will just sort of sneak up on you."

I looked at Sandra with surprise. "You mean you're really not confident all the time?"

Sandra smiled at me. "Not hardly, Kimmy."

"I always think of you as the most confident person I know."

"Let's face it, Kim, you don't know me very well," Sandra pointed out.

"That's true," I admitted. Then I forced myself to be brave enough to add "but I'd like to."

She gave me an appraising look. "I'll keep that in mind."

"So, listen," Savy said, jumping up from the bed. "How about if we go buy Kimmy some makeup, and then go over to Dangerous Threads?"

"I'm in," Jane agreed.

"We can all go in my Jeep," Sandra suggested.

"Well ... okay!" I agreed. I couldn't help smiling. I just felt so happy! I had these three incredible friends, and the band was going to be great, and I looked cute for maybe the first time in my life, and—

Beep-beep-beep.

Everyone looked over at my purse, which I had thrown on the dresser.

"It's, uh, my beeper," I explained awkwardly, heading for my purse. I don't know why I bothered to answer. I was sure it was my mother. The only other person who had the beeper number was my father, but he rarely used it.

Sure enough, my mother's number appeared in the little space on the beeper. I saw Jane and Savy trade looks, but I pretended not to notice. "I have to call my mom," I told them.

"Use my phone," Savy said. "We'll wait for you downstairs."

"Thanks," I said, as they filed out the door. I quickly dialed my mom's private number.

"Lilith Carrier," my mother answered crisply.

"You rang?" I asked drolly.

"Don't take that tone with me, young lady," my mother said. "I was concerned about you."

"I slept at Daddy's last night," I reported patiently. "Now I'm at band practice. I told you I'd be at band practice on Sunday."

"Did you go to church with your father this morning?" she asked me.

Since the divorce they went to different churches.

"Yes," I said, which was the truth. Believe me, it is a family rule that a Carrier not seen in church on Sunday morning is a dead Carrier.

"You could have come with me," my mother said.

"But I was at Dad's," I said, shaking my

head at the sheer stupidity of the conversation. "Did you beep me to ask me about church?"

"Kimberly, you have gotten increasingly quarrelsome lately, and I can't say it's an attractive quality," my mother said in her soft southern-tinged voice. "You never used to be difficult, so I can only assume it has to do with the company you keep."

There it was again. That veiled bigotry.

"Assume away," I told her breezily.

I heard her quick intake of breath. My mother was right. I never used to talk to her this way. It felt good. Scary, but good.

"I plan to send Mr. Gruller to fetch you," my mother said. "I'd like to see you this evening."

"I'm busy," I told her.

I knew she'd be shocked. After all, I was almost never busy. All I ever did was go to Savy's or spend hours in my room either doing homework or practicing guitar.

"This is not optional, Kimberly," my mother said in her frostiest voice.

"And you aren't the pope, so I know this isn't a command performance," I shot back.

I don't know where I found the nerve.

"I'm ashamed of you," she said in a small, tight voice. "Never in this life would I have talked to my mother that way."

And I did feel a little ashamed. Being well mannered had been bred into me from my first curtsy. "I'm sorry," I admitted. "It's just that I hate it when you beep me. No one else has a mother who beeps her."

"As you well know, our situation is different," my mother said stiffly.

As I well knew. But I was so very tired of it. And I was tired of trying to blend into the woodwork just to try to compensate for being different.

"But I really am busy tonight," I told my mother. "The band is going to look for stage outfits. I promised I'd go."

She sighed again. "Please make sure what you wear in public is in good taste, Kimberly."

"I'll keep that in mind," I said with mock solemnity. I caught a glimpse of the new me in the mirror. My mother would say I looked cheap and tacky. But I didn't.

My mother relented. "All right. Just please promise me you'll always be with a group and that someone will drive you right to our gate so the guard can watch you come in."

"I promise," I said, gritting my teeth hard. "I have to go now."

"Well, good night, then," my mother said.

"Good night," I replied softly, and hung up. I stood up and looked at myself again in the mirror. I *could* look pretty. I *could* take chances. And even if I didn't feel confident, I could act *as if*.

This was the beginning of the new me. And as the new me, I would not look at myself through my mother's eyes.

CHAPTER
5

(logo)

"Are you sure this is okay, Kimmy?" Savy asked doubtfully as we stood at the checkout counter at Dangerous Threads.

We were next in line, and heaped on the counter was a stage outfit and boots for each of us. I was about to pay for three of the outfits with my handy-dandy credit card.

"Sure I'm sure," I told her.

"My mom would kill me if she knew I borrowed money from you," Savy whispered to me anxiously. "And Gramma Beth would tan my hide, as she so quaintly puts it."

"So don't tell them!" I replied, acting *as if* I were utterly carefree.

It was the new me.

Hadn't I actually gone out of Savy's house

with the catsuit and baby-doll dress on? Hadn't I left all the makeup on my face? And hadn't I just let my friends talk me into picking out a wild stage outfit to wear when we made our debut that very Friday night?

Oh, God. I was scared to death.

But, no. That was the old Kimmy.

A fine guy in a fringed leather jacket walked by and smiled at me. At least, I think he was fine. I had my glasses packed away in my purse, and everything looked a little blurry. I tried to smile back in a cute way, but it may have looked more like a grimace.

Well, at least I was trying.

"It's this whole new experience going out with you in your stone-fox guise," Jane said, watching the cute guy check me out from behind a display of embroidered western shirts.

"It feels kind of ... funny," I admitted. "Like I'm wearing a costume."

"Everyone wears some kind of costume every day just to get out the front door," Sandra said philosophically. "It all just depends on how well the costume works."

The willowy girl behind the counter totaled up what I'd spent: $873.00 for my outfit, Savy's, and Jane's. Sandra insisted on paying for her own. I handed the girl my credit card and looked down at the outfits spilling over each other on the counter.

I got nervous all over again.

Jane, Savy, and Sandra had talked me into choosing an outfit consisting of black jeans and a fringed silver sleeveless top that bared my midriff. I had never worn anything like that in my life. My mother would faint dead away if she saw me in it. But then, there was zero chance my mother would come to hear Wild Hearts play.

Jane had also picked black jeans, and with them she'd be wearing a sheer silver and black western-cut shirt over a black bra top. Savy's outfit was a black denim miniskirt with an oversized sheer black shirt with silver buttons and a silver belt. And Sandra had bought a fitted black denim minishift with a bolero-cut black and silver jacket. We'd all picked out identical black cowboy boots with silver tips.

I signed the credit card slip, then Sandra paid for her outfit, and we were out the door with the loot.

"I love what we got," Savy said happily. "We are going to look so cute!"

"The important thing is that we are going to sound so good," Jane reminded us as we walked toward Sandra's Jeep. "I don't want anyone to ever say about us, 'They're good, for a girls' band.'"

"I wonder who's playing at the Exit-Inn tonight," Sandra said as we walked by the club.

"Let's go in," I said impetuously. I didn't want to go home to face my mother.

"I've got two hours of homework I need to get done," Sandra said.

"Oh, come on, just for a few minutes," I wheedled.

"We have to go in," Savy said. "Just to witness the reaction to the new Kimmy!"

"I really can't," Sandra insisted. "I've got to ace this history test."

"A half hour?" I begged.

We could hear music streaming out of the club, and it sounded good.

"Oh, okay," Sandra finally relented. "But only a half hour, I mean it. Anybody who bitches to stay longer than a half hour has to find her own way home."

The handmade sign at the front door said "Open band night. No cover."

"What does that mean?" I asked.

"It means any band can play," Jane said. "Haven't you ever been to a club on open band night before?"

"Not really," I replied honestly.

The room was noisy, rowdy, and crowded,

and we worked our way through the bodies until we could see the stage.

And right up there was Wyatt Shane, with his band, Thunder Rolls.

"Oh, great," Sandra groaned. "Instead of studying I'm watching this fool."

Someone else was playing lead guitar, since Wyatt's arm was still in a cast from his accident with Jane's mom's car. But Wyatt was singing.

"I'd like to stomp his face," Jane seethed, her eyes narrowed. "I'd like to break his other arm and both his legs."

"Yuck," I replied with a shiver. Of course, I couldn't blame her for feeling that way. Wyatt had gotten drunk, tried to put the heavy moves on Jane, and then taken off in her mother's car, abandoning Jane in the middle of nowhere! Then he'd gotten into a car accident, and *then* he'd blamed the whole thing on Jane, saying it was her fault for being such a tease!

"I can't even listen to this," Jane yelled over the loud music. "I'm going to the can."

"I'll go with you," I offered, and we headed for the ladies' room.

As we made our way through the crowd I couldn't help noticing that guys were looking at me differently than they usually did. Actually, the difference was that they actually *were* looking at me. I tugged self-consciously at the neckline of Savy's baby-doll dress. Everything felt so strange.

"Hey, Kimmy!" a voice called out to me from the crowd. I turned around, and even with my blurry vision I could see it was Dave Mallone. No one else looked quite like him. The dark lighting made his pale skin look yellow and sickly. I looked around for Jane, but she hadn't realized I'd stopped and she continued on toward the ladies' room.

"Well, hi," I said. I guess my surprise at seeing quiet, shy Dave Mallone at a rock club showed in my voice.

"I like clubs," he said in my ear, and then gave me his shy smile. "No one expects me to make conversation here."

I smiled back at him. "It's kind of tough to," I agreed in a loud voice. "Well, nice to see you," I added, and turned toward the ladies' room.

"Wait!" Dave called, touching my arm. I turned back to him. "You look different!" he yelled.

I smiled and shrugged my best oh-well-you-know patented meaningless shrug.

Thunder Rolls finished their song, and the crowd applauded.

"You're not wearing your glasses," Dave

said. I could hear him much better in the brief reprieve between songs.

"Um ..."

"It looks great."

"Oh, thanks," I managed. I felt flustered and so went to automatically push my nonexistent glasses up my nose. All I reached was nose bone. I pretended I had to scratch an itch.

"That dress is ..." Dave began. He looked down at my legs, legs no one at school had ever seen. "Short," he finished.

I blushed. "Um, yes, well, I have to go—"

"No, wait!" he pleaded.

I waited.

"Well, see, we both love music. Did you know that?"

"Mmmmmm," I managed.

"So ... how about if we go hear music together some time?" Dave asked hopefully, blinking those pale rabbity eyelashes at me.

Oh, no. He was asking me out again. Why couldn't he magically turn into Sawyer Paxton? Why did it have to be Dave Mallone who had a crush on me? And how could I turn him down without hurting his feelings when he hadn't said when exactly he wanted to go out with me? I couldn't tell him I was busy for the rest of my life. And I couldn't find it in my heart to tell him the truth—that I just wasn't interested.

"Gee, I'm really busy with the new band," I finally said.

"Oh, you know, it could be after band practice or whatever," Dave pressed. He giggled nervously and looked at me with such hope shining from those pale eyes that I couldn't bring myself to just say no. After all, he felt about me the way I felt about Sawyer.

"Maybe sometime," I said evasively. "I have to go now—"

"How about tomorrow?" Dave asked.

"Tomorrow?"

Dave nodded.

"Tomorrow is Monday," I said.

Dave nodded.

"I'm ... not allowed to go out on school nights." I'd invented that excuse. Actually I had no idea what either of my parents would say, since I'd never been invited on a date I wanted to go on.

"Next weekend, then," Dave pressed.

"I'm busy with the band," I replied with a smile that I hoped was kind and friendly but not too encouraging.

Dave's face kind of crumpled inward. I felt so bad for him. He knew what I knew. He might be a geek, but he wasn't stupid. If he'd been Sawyer Paxton I would have sneaked out my window and climbed down the trellis to be with him, instead of coming up with lame excuses.

"I'm sorry, Dave," I added, touching his hand gently.

"Oh, it's okay," he said, even though of course it wasn't.

Thunder Rolls started their next song, and I escaped toward the ladies' room. Jane was just coming out.

"What happened to you?" she asked me over the music.

"I ran into Dave Mallone," I yelled back.

"Is he the guy who looks like a rabbit?" she asked me.

I nodded. "He's nice, but ... you know," I said.

"Yeah," she replied knowingly. "No chemistry." She looked over her shoulder at the stage, where Wyatt Shane was singing a slow tune with his eyes closed. He looked very fine. "On the other hand, what you think is chemistry can get you into a lot of trouble, so what do I know?"

"Hey, what the hell are you doing here?" a harsh female voice rumbled from behind us.

Jane and I both turned around. And there was Wyatt's girlfriend, Brenda Pirkell.

Brenda had heard that Jane had gone out with Wyatt, and she'd shown up at school the night of the play ready to kick Jane's ass. Brenda is really tall and really big and really nasty-looking. She has tattoos. Savy, Sandra, and I had all rallied around Jane, which is what prevented some major bloodshed.

And here we were, face to face with the mean giant again.

"We were just leaving," Jane said, sidestepping Brenda. I sidestepped with her.

Brenda put a meaty arm on Jane's shoulder and stopped her. "What did I tell you about hanging around my guy?"

Jane sighed. "Look, I have no interest in your guy, okay? The two of you make a lovely couple. I hope you're real happy together." She shook Brenda's hand off of her and started to walk away.

Brenda spun her around. "You have one smart-ass mouth on you. I don't like your attitude."

"I don't really give a flying fig what you like," Jane said, staring Brenda down.

I closed my eyes and said a quick prayer. Why couldn't Jane learn the fine art of being a southern girl really, really fast so she could worm her way out of this sort of thing? A true southern belle would just drawl "Bless your heart" and be out of there.

"Well, you better care what I like," Brenda said, "if you want to live."

"Excuse me, but have you watched a few too many late-night gangster movies?" Jane asked. "I mean, who writes your dialogue?"

I pulled on Jane's shirt. "We were just leaving," I told Brenda with a sweet, conciliatory grin.

One of Brenda's friends, even taller than Brenda with bigger hair—which was a feat that defied certain laws of nature—came up next to Brenda.

"You want to take these wusses on, Bren?" she asked, crushing a beer can in her hand.

Jane looked at the girl's bulging biceps. "Hey, just a friendly suggestion, lay off the steroids, they're a killer."

"Jane!" I whispered harshly, but it was too late. Now the other girl was mad, too. She put one hand around Jane's neck and the other around mine. We were as captive as two butterflies impaled on pins.

"What should we do with the snot-rags?" the girl asked conversationally.

"I say we rock their world," Brenda decided. She started pushing us toward a back door.

"You can't do this!" Jane yelled. "Help!"

she screamed. But the club was so noisy and crowded no one even noticed.

Jane and I struggled and screamed as Brenda and her Amazon friend pushed us toward the door. What we were doing could have passed for dancing in there. No one paid us any mind.

Just as we got to the door—and I figured our lives were as good as over—there stood Dave Mallone.

"Hey, aren't you Thunder Rolls' manager?" he asked Brenda.

"No, I'm Wyatt Shane's girlfriend," Brenda replied.

"Wow, you really know those guys?" he asked, not looking at Jane and me at all.

"Yeah, so?" Brenda asked sullenly.

"So I think Thunder Rolls is the best band in Nashville, no lie," Dave said earnestly. "I was hoping I could book them for this big party out at Johnny Cash's house next month."

Brenda and her friend stood there, looking at Dave.

"You don't know Johnny Cash," Brenda's friend finally said. Her death grip on the back of my neck loosened a little.

"That's true," Dave admitted. "But I work for the guy who's booking talent for this party.

And he asked me to find the hottest rock band in town."

"Why would Johnny Cash want to hear rock when he sings country?" Brenda asked, her beady little eyes narrowed to slits.

"Hey, think about it," Dave said solemnly. "If you were a country legend, would you want some young country stars stealing the limelight at your party?"

Brenda and her friend looked at each other. "I guess not," Brenda finally said. She turned back to Dave. "I really like Johnny Cash, you know?"

"Oh, great, you'll have to come to the party!" Dave said. "You got some paper and a pen? I'll write down some info for you and you can have the band get in touch with me."

Brenda and her buddy scrambled in their purses for paper and pens. Here was our chance. Jane and I ran off into the crowd, as far away from Brenda and the other big-haired giantess as we could get.

"It's a good thing you're here, because we were just about to leave without you," Sandra said as Jane and I ran panting up to her. "How could you guys be so inconsiderate? I said a half hour and—"

"Shut up and head for the door!" Jane shouted.

"What is she talking about?" Savy asked me.

In the midst of the crowd I caught a glimpse of Brenda and company headed my way, murder still written across their Neanderthal brows.

"Run!" was my only suggestion.

Jane and I took off, and Sandra and Savy followed close behind. We made it to Sandra's Jeep just as Brenda and her buddy reached the corner.

"It's Wyatt's girlfriend!" Savy exclaimed, remembering Brenda from the confrontation at school. We all scrambled into the Jeep. "Wow, she looks even madder now than she did when she wanted to beat Jane up."

"Well, she still wants to beat Jane up," Jane said, "and all Jane's little friends, so gun the Jeep!"

Sandra wasted no time in starting the Jeep and heading it down the street. I turned around to see Brenda and the other girl giving us the finger.

"What the hell happened?" Sandra asked us.

"Brenda thought I was there to see Wyatt," Jane explained. "She decided my face should be rearranged."

"How'd ya'll get away from her?" Savy asked, wide-eyed.

"We were saved by Dave Mallone," I reported, finally letting my head fall back against the seat.

Savy thought a minute. "Dave Mallone who looks like a rabbit and has a crush on you?"

I nodded. "One and the same."

"He was at the club?" Sandra asked, looking at me in her rearview mirror.

"Yep," I replied. "He asked me out, I turned him down, and then he saved Jane and me from total destruction."

"Dang!" Savy marveled. "I didn't know the boy had it in him!"

"Now I feel completely guilty that I turned him down," I said with a sigh. I fumbled in my purse and put on my glasses. Suddenly the world came back into sharp focus.

"We do owe him a major thank-you," Jane allowed.

"Maybe I should just go out with him," I said with a sigh. The thought that my very first date would be with Dave Mallone was really depressing.

"That's ridiculous," Sandra said flatly, stopping the Jeep at a red light. "You can't thank a guy by going out on a date."

"Wouldn't it be . . . kind?" I asked them, searching for the right word.

"Nope," Jane said. "It would be a mercy date, seriously sucky."

"So what do we do, then?" I asked.

"We're southern," Savy said with a laugh in her voice. "We write him a thank-you note!"

Savy meant it as a joke, but that's exactly what I did.

CHAPTER
6

♡

K immy?"

It was the next day at school, and I was just taking some books out of my locker during my lunch break. I was back to looking like my normal self, which is to say drab. It's not that I hadn't enjoyed my transformation; I just wasn't ready to pull it off at school. I figured everyone would whisper about me, the pastel people would talk about me behind cupped hands, and I'd feel so self-conscious I would want to die.

But now here was Sawyer Paxton standing next to my locker, waiting to talk to me, and in that moment I fervently wished I looked the way I had the night before.

"Hi," I said, awkwardly shifting the books to my other arm.

"So, what's shakin'?" he asked me in a friendly voice, casually leaning against the locker next to mine.

"Oh, not much," I managed, trying a small smile on for size. Inside, my heart was beating a zillion miles per hour. Was he really just leaning there against the locker to ask me what was shaking? Did he care? And could that possibly lead to—oh, please, God—him asking me out on an actual date?

"So, listen," Sawyer continued, "I was thinking about doing my demo this Wednesday. Remember you said you might could play on it?"

I nodded. Sawyer could even make the fractured grammar of "might could" sound cute and original. Unfortunately he was only talking to me because he wanted me to play on his demo, not because he wanted to ravish my bony body.

"I know it's not much notice," he apologized, "but my dad's been in our studio rerecording some tracks, and Wednesday is the first night it's free."

"You have your own recording studio?" I asked him.

He nodded. "Out back of our house." He pulled a lead sheet out of his notebook and handed it to me. "This is the tune."

I took the lead sheet and glanced at the title.

"Perfect." Sure. It was about some girl who was beautiful and confident, the kind of girl Sawyer would like. What could I possibly have been thinking?

"Did you ask Jane yet?" I remembered that he'd asked Jane to play drums on the demo before he even knew I played the guitar.

Sawyer shook his head no. "I was just going to head over to the cafeteria and try to find her."

"She told me she has to work at Uncle Zap's on Wednesday," I told Sawyer. "That's why we don't have band practice planned."

"Drag," Sawyer commented. "I guess I'll have to ask this other drummer I know, but he's not as good as Jane. She's really great, isn't she?"

"Yeah," I said softly and pushed my glasses up my nose. So it was Jane he wanted. Well, that made sense.

"Anyway, can you be at my house Wednesday night at, like, seven?" Sawyer asked me. He scribbled down his address and handed it to me.

"Sure," I said, and tucked his address into my purse.

"Thanks," he replied with a boyish grin. "I sure do appreciate it. Catch ya later."

I turned and wistfully watched him walk

away. He looked just as good going as he did coming.

"Maybe you should wipe the drool off your face," Jane suggested, sidling up beside me.

"Oh, hi," I said laconically. I turned back to catch Sawyer rounding the corner. "He was looking for you."

"For real?" Jane asked.

"He wanted us both to play on his demo Wednesday night. I told him I though you had to work."

"I switched my shift to Wednesday afternoon so we could rehearse later on, since Friday is the big night," Jane informed me.

"Don't remind me," I groaned. "And I just told him I'd do his demo!"

"Aren't you guys eating?" Sandra asked us on her way to the lunchroom.

"Hey, can we practice Wednesday night?" Jane asked Sandra.

She walked back over to us. "You said you had to work."

"Well, now I don't," Jane said.

"I've got a tennis match," Sandra said. "I only said I'd play then because you said you were working. I can't change it now."

"Okay, don't," Jane said with a shrug. "We'll just have to really, really work hard every other night between now and Friday."

She turned to me with a grin. "And you and I are gonna get to play in Judd Paxton's recording studio!"

"I gotta run," Sandra said. "I've got student council stuff to do. See you in the cafeteria."

Jane and I started walking slowly toward the lunchroom.

"Do you think Sawyer's cute?" I asked Jane timidly.

"Yeah, I guess," Jane said. We rounded the corner. "You've got good taste, Kimmy."

"Well, he isn't interested in me," I informed her. "He's interested in you."

"Get out of town," Jane scoffed.

"It's true," I informed her. "You should have seen the look on his face when he talked about you. He was practically swooning."

"For real?" she asked me. "Huh. Well, I'm not really interested in him, Kimmy."

"But why not?" I wondered. "I would pull white off rice to get him to like me."

Jane smiled at me. "That's exactly why. You want him, and the girls of Wild Hearts never go after each other's guys."

A couple of the more hateful pastel people were going by us in the opposite direction. They turned their faces away from us and went "Quack-quack," which was their way of making fun of Jane. You see, one truly evil girl named Katie Lynn Kilroy had started the rumor that Jane was, well, slutty. And even though it was totally untrue, Jane was too proud to refute the rumor. So one day Katie Lynn said to Jane: "If it walks like a duck and talks like a duck"—meaning that if Jane acted tough and experienced, it must mean she really was fast and loose. Ever since that day the pastel people have been quacking whenever Jane walks by.

"I don't know how you can take that," I said, looking at Jane out of the corner of my eye. "You are so calm. I would just up and die."

"Please," Jane snorted.

Of course, I knew it bothered Jane more than she let on—she'd confided that to all the girls in the band one night. Still, she had acting *as if* down to a science.

I sighed. "Well, I just wish I could be more like you."

"Sure," Jane said easily. "Want to borrow the uni?"

I looked over at the bowling shirt she had on, which she'd once informed me she'd acquired at Goodwill for a dollar. The name embroidered on the breast pocket was Chuckie. A plastic bowling-pin barrette held back her hair on one side. She even had on bowling shoes—I don't know where she found them.

"Thanks, but no thanks," I replied.

"Oh, come on, Kimmy, loosen up," Jane chided me. "How come you look like your old self again today, anyway?"

I shrugged. "I can't come to school like that."

"Like what?" Jane asked, as we pushed open the doors to the crowded cafeteria. "Wearing makeup and cute clothes?"

"It's just too big of a leap," I explained.

Jane shrugged. "Suit yourself." We both saw Savy sitting with Sandra and waved. Then we got in the food line. "Just keep in mind that everyone isn't looking at you all the time. Like, most kids probably wouldn't even notice if you looked different. They're too busy obsessing about their own problems."

We got our food—a tuna plate for me, and a burger and fries for Jane—and headed over to Savy and Sandra.

"There's Sawyer," I said, cocking my head toward the other side of the room.

"Back in a flash," Jane said, popping a fry into her mouth on the run.

"Don't they look cute together?" I asked Sandra and Savy as I watched Sawyer and Jane across the room.

"He likes you, not her," Savy told me, taking a huge bite out of a homemade chicken breast, compliments of Gramma Beth.

"He doesn't," I sighed, mushing some tuna around on my plate.

"The power of positive thinking seems to be a concept lost on you," Sandra said dryly, sipping her fruit juice.

"Sorry," I whispered. "I know I'm boring."

"I'm outta here," Sandra said, getting up. "When you start on this 'poor me' stuff, Kimmy, I just cannot stand it."

"Don't leave!" I protested. "I'm sorry!"

"I have to go run some papers off for the student council meeting," Sandra said, picking up her tray. "So don't take it personally."

"She hates me," I told Savy when Sandra left.

"You know that isn't true," Savy replied. She pretended to pull hard on my hair. "What happened to yesterday's Kimmy, the cute, confident one?"

"I washed my hair and scrubbed off the makeup," I said with a shrug.

"Uh-uh, something else," Savy said, looking at me contemplatively. "Why do I have a feeling this has something to do with your mother?"

I sighed. Savy had known my mother forever, and she knew we didn't get along. In fact, as far as I was concerned, my mother was responsible for most of the misery in my life, and this time was no exception.

I'd gone home the night before in Savy's pink dress. Usually I didn't run into my mother unless we planned to see each other—that's how big her house is. But the night before, she'd been coming down the front staircase just as I was going up.

"What is *that*?" she'd asked me, aghast.

"It's just a dress," I'd mumbled, suddenly feeling as if I were stark naked.

"Well, you look like a . . . a common street-walker, Kimberly," my mother had informed me, unable to disguise the disgust she felt.

"I don't think so," I'd said, forcing myself to look her in the eye. "I think I look nice."

"*Nice*?" She'd sniffed like I was chopped meat gone bad. "The young people you keep company with consider this *nice*?" Then she'd reached up and pulled violently at the neckline of Savy's dress. "Your bosom is hanging out, your skirt is indecent, and you look as if you just tumbled out of bed, which for all I know you just did!"

Tears of embarrassment had come to my eyes. She had never talked to me that way before in my life. I, who at the age of sixteen had to live with the excruciating knowledge that I hadn't yet been really kissed, was standing there with my own mother accusing me of sleeping around. It was just too awful for words.

Then she just turned away from me and went downstairs, and that was the last I'd seen of her until this morning, when I'd come down to breakfast as the old me.

Savy was and is my best friend. So I told her the whole story.

"Oh, Kimmy, she was totally wrong," Savy said earnestly, grabbing my hand from across the table and squeezing it hard.

"Yeah, but it's not worth the struggle," I said, gulping hard.

"Okay, everything's set," Jane said, striding back over to us. She took a big bite of her burger and washed it down with some Coke. "He said you had the lead sheet, and I should make a copy of yours," she added.

"Oh, yeah, I stuffed it in here somewhere," I said, opening my notebook. "Here it is." I handed the lead sheet to Jane.

She scanned it quickly. "Mondo country," she decided, wrinkling her nose. "Kinda sappy."

"You'd say that about any lyric that didn't

rhyme with 'nose ring,'" Savy told her, polishing off her chicken breast.

"What did you think?" Jane asked me.

"I haven't had a chance to read it yet, actually."

She handed it to me, and I read Sawyer's song.

PERFECT

Music and lyrics by Sawyer Paxton

Every day I see her, but so do other guys.
They just don't know how she looks in my eyes.
They don't see the things I see,
But that's okay, she's perfect to me.

My friends go for a wild look, a sexy style.
But I can see forever in her lovely smile.
They don't see the things I see,
But that's okay, she's perfect to me.

Oh, I would give up anything and everything
For just one chance to hold her close and let
my heart sing. . . .

Every day I see you, and so do other guys.
But they don't know how you look in my eyes.
They don't see the things I see,
But darling, you're perfect to me.

"Well, it is really country," I agreed. "Kind of old-style country at that."

"I rest my case," Jane said smugly.

"I love it," I sighed, holding the lead sheet reverently to my chest.

"Oh, you'd love it if he wrote the phone book," Jane snorted.

"But it's so romantic," I breathed. I looked at the lead sheet again. So there was some girl somewhere who had inspired Sawyer to write this song. Which meant Sawyer was in love.

But not with me.

It would never be me.

CHAPTER
7

No, no, no, and another no," I muttered to myself as I pawed through my boring wardrobe. Baggy shirt after baggy sweater after baggy skirt zoomed along the rack of my closet as I pushed every article of clothing that I owned behind me. Every article of clothing I owned that was at my mother's house, that is. I had a bunch of equally dull, baggy items sitting at my father's house in Green Hills.

It was Wednesday evening, and I was trying to get dressed for the demo session at Sawyer's. I wanted to look wonderful, but at the same time I was scared that if I tried to look wonderful all I'd end up looking like is one of those pathetic girls who try to look good but fail miserably and everyone just whispers about them and says how pathetic they are. So, if that was going to be the case, I reasoned that I'd be better off looking like someone who didn't try and didn't care.

A shrink could probably have had a good ole time with me.

Just as I worked my way to the very back of my closet, the phone rang. I have private unlisted numbers at both of my parents' homes. Trust me when I tell you my phone didn't ring very much.

"Hello?"

Nothing but the sound of heavy breathing.

I had been getting these weird heavy-breathing calls for the last couple of days. When I wasn't home, my answering machine had picked up a dozen, and I'd personally breathed back at the breather a dozen times or so.

"Look, please stop calling here or I will call the police." Why I was saying please is because I was brought up to say please. I just can't help it.

More breathing.

"I'm hanging up now," I told the breather. Then I did.

I went back to my hopeless closet.

The phone rang again.

"Hello?" I answered, more sharply this time.

The same stupid heavy breathing.

"I am going to get one of those whistles that burst eardrums, and I'm going to blow it into the phone the next time you call," I told the breather. Then I hung up again.

I wasn't scared about the calls. I remember in my psychology class the teacher once said that people who call and don't say anything are annoying but harmless, almost always too shy to be any threat to you.

And of course I didn't dare report it because then my mother would find out, and she would purely lose her mind and possibly never let me out of the house without a chaperon in my lifetime.

I checked my watch. It was already six o'clock, and Jane was due to pick me up at six-thirty. What was I going to wear? I stared at my hopeless closet. And there, at the very back, was the pink baby-doll dress and white lace cat suit Savy had lent me. I had planned on having the outfit dry-cleaned, which was why I hadn't returned it yet.

Without letting myself talk me out of it, I snatched it from the closet and threw it on the bed. Then I quickly slid into the cat suit and dropped the dress over my head. From the top shelf of my dresser I got out the little white bag of cosmetics that my friends had insisted I buy. I took off my glasses and slipped them into my purse, then I put on eyeliner—which came out all smudgy and I had to take most of it off—mascara, and lipstick. I brushed my hair from underneath and threw my head back so it was all full-looking, and then I sprayed myself with some perfume.

I looked kind of good. Maybe.

And my mother wasn't at home to tell me otherwise.

Br-i-i-i-ng!

I marched over to the telephone.

"I really mean it, stop calling here or you will get arrested and sent to prison!" I yelled into the phone.

"Wow, you must really hate phone calls," Jane's voice came back at me.

"Oh, hi," I said. "I thought you were someone else."

"Let me hazard a wild guess—someone you don't like?" Jane asked.

"Someone has been calling here and just breathing," I told her.

"Oh, a perv," she replied. "Mondo gross-out."

"No, he never says anything; he just breathes."

"Yeah, but what's he thinking?" Jane said darkly. "Anyway, we'll talk about the perv later. We've got a major problem. My car died. Can you get wheels?"

"I don't have a car!" I cried, sitting down hard on the bed. I had to get to Sawyer's, I just had to.

"A taxi, maybe?" Jane asked. "But we're doing this demo for free, so it seems kinda dumb. Not that I have any bucks, anyway."

"Neither do I," I said with a sigh. Like most really rich people, no one in my family ever keeps any cash in the house.

"We're screwed, then," Jane said flatly.

There was only one possibility.

"I could ask my mom's driver to take us," I said tentatively.

"Driver, as in chauffeur?" Jane asked.

"Uh-huh," I said meekly, fiddling nervously with the slender gold chain around my neck. "I mean, he could drop us near Sawyer's, so no one would know how we got there, and then—"

"Are you kidding?" Jane interrupted me. "Why would I care?"

"Oh, I guess you wouldn't," I replied.

"So, cool," Jane exclaimed. "See you in a few."

I hung up and then dialed the extension to Mr. and Mrs. Gruller's cottage behind my mother's house.

"Yes?" Mrs. Gruller answered the phone.

"Hi, it's Kimmy," I said, twisting the phone cord around my finger. "Do you think Mr. Gruller could drive my friend and me somewhere?"

"I believe your mother drove herself to her meeting, so he's free," Mrs. Gruller said. "I'll have him bring the car around, all right?"

"Thanks," I told her, and hung up.

Okay. So Jane and I were going to Sawyer's in my mom's chauffeur-driven Rolls, which was excruciating.

Maybe Jane didn't care, but I certainly did.

"We're looking for Otter Creek; it's right off Franklin," Jane said, reading the direction off a piece of paper. "Then we should see a sign that says Shadow Wood."

"That a subdivision?" Mr. Gruller asked from the front seat.

"No, it's his family's estate," I explained.

"Silly me," Mr. Gruller teased.

"There it is," Jane said, pointing to the street sign.

Mr. Gruller turned onto Otter Creek, a narrow street that led to a well-known nature preserve. We came to a narrow road off to the left, where one side read Private Drive and the other read Shadow Wood.

"Bingo," Jane declared. She looked at her watch as Mr. Gruller drove the Rolls up the private drive. "And we're even on time."

"Uh, would you mind stopping the car here?" I asked Mr. Gruller.

He was used to my strangeness regarding arriving á la chauffeured auto, so he just said, "Sure," and stopped the car.

Jane looked at me. "You're kidding."

I blushed. "It's less ostentatious, isn't it?"

"Kimmy, first of all, if Sawyer is peeking out the window to see how we arrive, which I sincerely doubt, then he'll see us walk up from his private drive. That will provoke a question, such as 'What did you do, hitch?,' which we will have to answer. And second of all, we're at an estate so big it has a name. The people who live here don't care about the chauffeur thing."

"Oh, yes, they would," I said earnestly. "No offense, but you don't understand because you're not from here. No one in country music has a chauffeur, isn't that right, Mr. Gruller?"

"Got me," Mr. Gruller replied. "I listen to jazz."

"Well, trust me, I'm right. They all drive Explorers."

"Fine, I don't know and I don't care," Jane informed me, reaching for the door handle.

"But I gotta tell you, Kimmy, sometimes it's very difficult to follow the strange twists your mind takes."

"For me, too," I agreed, getting out of the car on my side before Mr. Gruller could open it for me.

"You want me to wait for you?" Mr. Gruller asked, sticking his head out of his window.

"No, thanks, I'll call you if we need a ride back, okay?"

"You got it," Mr. Gruller agreed, and backed the car back down the driveway.

Jane and I walked and walked and walked. The house was still not in sight.

"Oh, very bright, Kimmy," Jane groused as we tramped up the endless driveway. "Why do all you people have so much land, can you answer me that? Why can't you live on top of each other like normal people do?"

I didn't bother answering.

After another five minutes of walking, we finally caught sight of the house. It was huge. And far away. On top of a really, really large hill.

"Oops," I said, cringing. "I'm really sor—"

"Don't say one more word," Jane warned me. "Don't apologize. Don't even open your mouth."

We tramped up the narrow dirt driveway—I

guess it was supposed to look rustic or discourage tourists or something—and finally reached the wide front porch that ran along the front of the huge red-brick mansion. My white clogs were covered with dirt, and a bramble had caught the lace at the bodice of the catsuit, tearing a small hole. I looked at Jane. Her face was covered with dirt and sweat, and a caterpillar was crawling in her hair.

Jane raised her fist to knock on the door, but I quickly grabbed her hand. "No, wait! We have to get cleaned up first! I can't let Sawyer see me like this!"

Jane gave me a look that could've killed. "I am not going to be even later than I already am because you want to get gussied up, or whatever it is you southern belles do."

"I'm hardly a southern belle," I said with dignity.

"Ask me if I care," Jane replied, and she pounded on the front door.

Sawyer swung the heavy white door open himself. "Hey! I thought maybe ya'll forgot about me!" he exclaimed, ushering us into the cavernous front hall. Then he noticed the state we were in. "Uh, what happened?"

"We thought the house was near the road, so we got dropped off," Jane explained, pushing some hair out of her face.

The caterpillar fell from her hair onto the heavy white carpeting of the entrance hall.

"There's a guest bathroom right down that hall," Sawyer said, as he watched the caterpillar crawl around the carpet. He pointed to the right. "When you're through, we'll be in the studio. Just go out the sliding glass doors and walk across the backyard, okay?"

"Okay," I agreed, and Jane and I escaped to the bathroom.

I looked even worse than I had feared. There was a dead bug on my right cheek. Mascara had mixed with sweat, and it kind of drooled down under one eye. My pouffed-up hair had gone all flat. "Do I look as awful as I think I look?" I wailed.

"Worse," was Jane's retort. "You can't really tell without your glasses."

I scrambled through my purse for my glasses, hoping to see to repair the damage.

"I was kidding," Jane informed me. "You look fine—or you will if you just wash your face. That dead bug is kinda gross."

I looked in the mirror again. "Oh, Lord, Sawyer saw me with a dead bug on my face!"

"And he's gonna see you with a fat lip if you don't wash your face and get your butt out of this bathroom," Jane threatened, as she splashed water on her own face. We're here to play music, not to win a beauty contest."

"But—"

Jane folded her arms—her best I-am-not-kidding pose. "I rue the day we did that makeover on you, Kimmy, I really do."

She was so angry with me there was no use in my protesting. I just washed quickly and followed her out of the bathroom.

We crossed the yard—it was beautiful, with a brook, large fruit trees, and colorful hammocks swaying in the slight breeze—until we came to the wooden A-frame building that was the recording studio.

"Sorry to keep you guys waiting," Jane said, as she swung open the door.

"No prob," Sawyer said easily. He had been playing pool on a miniature table in the corner with a guy I'd never seen before.

I quickly took in the awards and laminated articles that covered the walls. There were more than two dozen gold or platinum albums, awards from the Academy of Country Music and from the Country Music Association, two Grammys, and even a cover from *Rolling Stone.*

"Wow," I breathed, overwhelmed.

"My dad," Sawyer said simply. He gave me a boyish grin that melted my heart. "That's

Keifer Washington," Sawyer said, cocking his head at the handsome, slender African American guy shooting the eight ball into the side pocket. "Keifer goes to the University School. He's a great bass player."

"Hey," Keifer said, not looking up from his pool shot.

"And this is Jane McVay, a kick-ass drummer, and Kimmy Carrier, hot lead guitar."

Keifer stood up and looked me over. "You play lead?"

I nodded.

"Huh," was all he said.

I immediately felt insecure. Was that a "huh" as in "I don't believe you're any good"? Why did one little "huh" make me doubt myself so quickly?

"So, did ya'll get a chance to look over my lead sheet?" Sawyer asked us.

"Straight-ahead country," Jane commented. "No biggie."

Sawyer looked at me.

"I think I'm okay with it," I said nervously, though right at that moment I wasn't sure I remembered how to play the guitar at all.

"Great," Sawyer replied. "Uh, where's your guitar?"

My guitar. I hadn't brought my guitar.

"I, uh, I . . ." I stammered.

"She didn't want to lug it," Jane improvised quickly. "We figured for sure you had one she could use."

"My dad's got four, but this is the only one he keeps here," Sawyer said reluctantly, walking over to a guitar in the corner. "He'll kill me if he finds out we used it. I only play keyboards myself."

He opened the weathered guitar case and pulled out an old Stratocaster. I turned my head sideways and read the signature scrawled on the body of the guitar: Elvis Presley.

"Elvis actually signed this?" I managed to squeak.

"My dad used to play with him," Sawyer explained. He held out the guitar. "In fact, Elvis even played this baby a time or two."

I was about to play a guitar that Elvis had played.

"Oh, no, I couldn't—" I protested.

"Hey, it's okay," Sawyer assured me. "My dad is out of town; he'll never know."

"No, I mean, Elvis played it—"

Sawyer gave me that grin of his again. "It's really okay, Kimmy."

"Yeah, rumor has it Elvis is dead," Jane said deadpan.

"I don't know. My grandmother insists he's still working undercover for the CIA," Keifer put in, setting his pool cue into the holder on the wall.

"Sure, with Marilyn Monroe," Jane added solemnly.

"Yeah, they're both going on diets and then they're making a big duet comeback album," Keifer concluded.

"I don't care what ya'll say," I managed. "Elvis was the King. And I can't play his guitar."

I saw Jane and Keifer trade looks, but I didn't care.

"Kimmy, the King would be proud to know a musician as good as you played this guitar," Sawyer said solemnly.

I felt a little thrill of happiness course down my spine.

Okay, I knew I was being a wuss. One minute I felt hopelessly insecure and the next I felt like a gazillion bucks just because Sawyer had complimented me. Sandra says I'm not self-actualized, which is one of those words made up by therapists on talk shows who are hawking their latest book.

I took the guitar and held it reverently.

Sawyer took a step toward me. "You've got a little something on your cheek," he said softly. Then his knuckles brushed gently against my skin. "Just some dirt or something," he added, looking right into my eyes.

He was flirting with me.

But he couldn't be flirting with me.

Because he liked Jane.

Didn't he?

"That was great!" Sawyer said when we'd recorded his demo for the fifth time. "Let me just play it back and make sure it's a keeper."

He rewound the tape, and we listened intently to the four tracks we'd just laid down.

"Sounds good," Keifer agreed, nodding. He looked over at me. "You are a hellified guitar player," he added.

I blushed. "Thanks."

"Where did you learn that blues riff?"

I shrugged. "I just copied off of records I like, I guess."

"Listen, I can't thank ya'll enough for this," Sawyer said. "I promise next time I'll pay for your time."

"Promises, promises!" Jane said with a laugh. She came out from behind the drums and stretched.

She looked so darling and confident. I saw both guys giving her admiring looks, and I imagined they must be thinking how cool she looked. I tried to copy her, but I felt ridiculous.

"Hey, I mean it!" Sawyer insisted. "Major

Bob Music called today about two of my songs. I think I'm really close to getting a publishing deal."

" 'Close' only counts in horseshoes," Keifer reminded him, slipping into his jean jacket.

"So I'm a dreamer," Sawyer said with a grin. "Hey, how about if I take ya'll out for a burger or something?" He looked at me. "Were you planning to call someone for a ride home?"

"Our cars are both on the fritz," I lied, "so I need to call—"

"Well, how about if we go get some food, and then I drive you ladies home?" Sawyer offered.

"As long as it's not Krystals," Keifer said, putting his bass guitar in its case. "No one can eat that stuff sober."

"Hey, I'm a big spender. We're talking Musical Burgers!" Sawyer said with a laugh. Musical Burgers is the hippest place in town for inexpensive food. It's open twenty-four hours, and all the musicians hang out there.

Then he casually draped his arm around my shoulders as we headed for the door.

I had played a guitar that Elvis had played.

I was going to Musical Burgers with Sawyer Paxton.

Oh, my God. It was my first date.

*   *   *

"I can't believe you did that!" I was laughing so hard that the Coke I was drinking practically came out of my nose.

We'd been at Musical Burgers for an hour, and had each devoured a huge burger and some fries.

Sawyer was sitting next to me, and Keifer was sitting next to Jane. Since Jane sat down first and Keifer had quickly slid into the booth next to her, I didn't know if Sawyer was sitting next to me because he didn't have any choice or because he wanted to. If he had only sat there because he had to, then I couldn't count it as my first date. On the other hand, if he'd wanted to sit with me all along, then I could.

These are the kinds of details I obsess about.

After a while I stopped thinking about it, though, because I was having such a great time. Various studio musicians who knew Sawyer through his dad came by and said hello. And Sawyer was telling us hilarious stories about all the trouble he'd gotten into when he was a kid hanging out at his dad's gigs. Like the time when he was six and he squirted ketchup from the little plastic fast-food packages into Willie Nelson's guitar.

"I really did that," Sawyer told us. "I had seen some late-night horror-movie thing where some guy's guitar got all bloody, so I decided to re-create the moment with ketchup!"

"What did Willie Nelson do?" Jane asked Sawyer.

"Nothing, because he never caught me," Sawyer replied. "When I saw the look on his face as that ketchup came oozing out of his guitar, I figured running was a good first choice."

"You were a little devil," Jane opined, finishing her last fry.

"You got that right," Sawyer agreed.

"And you aren't exactly a little angel now," Keifer added.

"See how my friends do me?" Sawyer asked, shaking his head ruefully.

"Poor baby," I teased.

Me, Kimmy Carrier, teasing Sawyer Paxton! If I stopped to think about it I'd lose all my nerve!

"Keifer over there just doesn't appreciate me for the sensitive guy I am," Sawyer said solemnly. "What I need is a lot of tender loving care."

Sawyer casually draped his arm over the back of the booth and reached under my hair to caress my neck. I was so psyched I barely allowed myself to breathe, but at the same time I wanted to make sure that the look on my face said it was no big thing.

Jane rolled her eyes and looked over at Keifer. "These sensitive types really make me want to hurl."

Keifer laughed. "I knew we had a lot in common." He toasted her with the last of his Coke.

I took this exchange in in a haze, because Sawyer's fingers were gently but firmly massaging the back of my neck. I closed my eyes and gave myself up to the feeling.

Bliss.

"Hi, Kimmy, long time no see!"

I opened my eyes, and there stood Dave Mallone, grinning nervously.

"Oh, hi, Dave," I said. "Ya'll know Dave? He's in our class. And this is Keifer Washington. He goes to USN."

"Hi," Dave said, bobbing his head up and down on his skinny, pale neck. "So, ya'll just hanging out?"

"Yep," Sawyer replied.

Dave didn't move. He just stood there.

"So . . . want to pull up a chair?" Sawyer finally asked.

"Oh, okay, sure," Dave agreed.

Like he hadn't been ready to stand at our

table for the millennium until someone invited him to join us.

"Wow, Kimmy, you look great," Dave said, staring at me.

"Thanks," I replied politely, wishing he would just go away.

Dave bit off a hangnail and then drummed his fingers on the table nervously. "Hey, did Kimmy tell you about what happened when she and I were at the Exit In the other night?"

I blushed. Dave made it sound as if I'd been out with him at the Exit In. But it would've been just too rude to correct him, after he'd saved Jane and me from the Tattooed Amazon Girls from Hell.

So Dave launched into an endless version of the story. Usually he never opened his mouth at all, but he told this story as if he'd been saving up words for about a century. He went into every minute detail that no one cared about, until finally all of us got so bored that we started yawning and Sawyer asked for the check.

Dave followed us up to the cash register. "So, how was your demo session tonight?" he asked me.

Jane gave him a sharp look. "How did you know we did a demo session?"

Dave's pale face got blotchy. "I, uh, I must have overheard you at school."

After Sawyer paid the check, we all stood around on the sidewalk in front of the restaurant.

"Nice to see you, Dave," Sawyer said politely.

"Oh, yeah, nice to run into ya'll," Dave agreed. "Hey, Kimmy, we'll have to go out again sometime, okay?"

"Dave, we never actually went out," I said in a low voice.

"Sure we did," Dave insisted.

"Hey, we gotta boogie," Jane put in loudly. "See ya, Dave."

"Oh, sure, well ... bye!" Dave called to us.

Jane propelled me toward Sawyer's car a few steps ahead of Sawyer and Keifer. Then Sawyer ran into a musician he knew and they stopped to talk.

"Thanks," I told her gratefully. "I feel so sorry for Dave, you know?"

"Don't bother," Jane snapped. "He's a very bizarro guy."

"No, he's just shy and lonely," I replied.

"I doubt it," Jane said. "Want to know what I think?"

"What difference does it make? You're going to tell me anyway."

Jane folded her arms and leaned close to me. "Here's a news flash for you, Kimmy. Betcha sweet Dave is the one who's been calling you and breathing."

"Dave?" I repeated. I had never thought about it before. Then I remembered he had my private phone number. I had given it to him when we were working on a science project together.

"Dave," Jane insisted. "And I'd suggest you stay far away from him."

"But he's as harmless as a flea," I protested. "And he doesn't really seem to have any friends."

"Cuz he's a major geek," Jane pointed out.

"A lot of people think I'm a major geek," I said defensively.

"I'm not talking about the idiotic pastel people," Jane snorted. "I'm talking truly weird. Kimmy, he knew we were doing that session tonight. And did you notice he was at Musical Burgers all by himself?"

"So?" I asked.

"So I think he followed us there," Jane concluded. "To see you."

CHAPTER
8

♡

I can't do it."

"Yes, you can!" Savy insisted.

"It's not such a biggie," Jane said.

"You cannot spend your life being such a wuss," Sandra added.

I sighed heavily.

It was Friday, and I was sitting in the cafeteria at school with Savy, Jane, and Sandra. That night was our big debut performance at the Juvenile Arthritis Foundation fund-raiser at the Opryland Hotel.

And my friends thought I should invite Sawyer.

Okay, I admit it. Every waking moment when I wasn't thinking about the band, I was thinking about him. He was nice to me at school, but he didn't seem to really seek me out or anything. And since I didn't have the nerve to wear anything except my usual baggy, drab clothes and my thick glasses and my hair stuck back in a limp ponytail, I figured he couldn't possibly see me as a *girl,* as in *girlfriend.*

"He obviously likes you," Jane said, sucking up the last of her milk shake.

"I am so sure," I drawled.

I snuck a look across the room where Sawyer was sitting with three of his friends. They were laughing about something.

Me? No, that was too paranoid. I wasn't going to be that way anymore. So I'd have to find another excuse.

"It's too late to ask him now," I told my friends.

"It's not," Savy insisted.

"It'll seem casual this way," Sandra pointed out.

"Shouldn't he ask me out before I ask him out?" I wondered.

"Girl, get your head out of the fifties," Sandra instructed.

"I wasn't even born in the fifties," I pointed out.

"I know you catch my drift, Kimmy," Sandra said, raising her eyebrows at me.

"He's looking at you," Savy told me casually.

"He is not."

"Is too," she insisted. "With a lot of interest, I might add."

Jane threw her napkin on the floor near me. "Could you get that for me, Kimmy?" she asked me innocently, cocking her head in Sawyer's direction so I'd get what I was really supposed to do—check him out while my head was under the table retrieving her napkin.

I bent down and took a look. He really *was* looking at me! Our eyes met—me with my head stuck under the table—and I felt like such an idiot that I straightened up quickly. Too quickly.

Oof. I banged my head hard on the underside of the table.

From across the room I heard Sawyer and his friends laughing.

Laughing!

I grabbed my books and headed for the door, too humiliated to even pay attention to my friends who were calling after me to come back.

"Hey, Kimmy, wait!"

I stopped dead in my tracks, but I didn't turn around.

It was Sawyer. He had come after me.

"I'm sorry we laughed," he told me. "But you really did look funny."

I stared at the floor and felt my glasses slipping down my nose.

"Come on, don't be mad," he urged me. He ducked his head down to catch my eye. "Please?"

"It doesn't matter," I managed to whisper.

"Hey, what happened to that fun girl I was out with the other night?" he asked me.

"I . . . I . . ."

"You can't let things freak you out so much, Kimmy," Sawyer said softly. "I mean, you're so talented, and so pretty, and such a great girl, but you're, like, scared of your own shadow!"

I straightened up quickly. "No, I'm not." I pressed my lips together hard, because of course what he was saying was true. Everyone knew it. Everyone thought it was just too hilarious.

Well, I wasn't laughing. I was sick of it.

I took a deep breath. "I mean, I used to be," I added, "but now I'm not."

"Good," Sawyer said with a grin.

This was the moment. It was do or die.

"I was wondering," I began. I looked him in the eye. Oh, God, too scary. I looked away again. "Well, Wild Hearts—the band I'm in—

we're playing at this charity thing tonight. And . . . I was wondering if you'd like to come."

"Gee, tonight?" Sawyer asked slowly.

"Oh, it's okay," I rushed in. "I know I didn't give you any notice." I started backing away from him. "I mean, you probably had something to do. Lots of stuff to do. So it's no big thing, I mean, I—"

"Yo, Kimmy, take five!" Sawyer interrupted with laughter. He took a few steps toward me to bridge the gap. "I'd love to come."

"You would?"

"Sure," he replied easily. "I bet ya'll are great. So, should I pick you up or meet you there?"

"Meet me," I decided. "The band is going together. Opryland Hotel, eight o'clock. Just ask where the Juvenile Arthritis fund-raiser is."

"Cool," Sawyer agreed. "See ya!" He turned around and walked away.

As for me, I couldn't move. I was rooted to the spot.

I had asked Sawyer Paxton out. And he had said yes.

My life was passing before my eyes.

I stood backstage in the huge ballroom at

the Opryland Hotel, and looked out at the sea of faces. Hundred and hundreds of faces.

Sure, they looked happy at the moment, because they were listening to Wynonna, as in Wynonna Judd, sing her latest hit.

Through some nightmarish fluke of timing—like that Wynonna had to leave early and board her tour bus to get to her next gig—she had gone on before us.

Yes. Wynonna was opening for Wild Hearts.

Sweat poured off of me. I looked over at Jane, Savy, and Sandra. They didn't look any too happy, either. Oh, they looked cute—really, really cute—in the outfits we'd bought at Dangerous Threads. But the fact that we were following Wynonna had everyone flipped out. Even Sandra.

"Look, we just do our best," she said in a voice loud enough to carry over Wynonna's rocking band.

"Her backup singers do choreography," Savy moaned, sounding miserable. She watched Wynonna's hot backup trio perform some intricate moves.

"Well, we don't need choreography," Jane insisted. "We are great. We're going to blow them away."

She sounded like she was trying to talk herself into this point of view.

"Excuse me. Which one of you is Kimmy?" a young volunteer asked.

"Me," I replied.

"Some guy gave me this for you," she told me, and handed me a folded slip of paper.

Wyatt! I opened the paper and read it. Fortunately the lettering was large enough for me to read it without my glasses. "Kimmy," it read, "I'm out here rooting for you. I know you will be awesome, because you *are* awesome! From Someone Who Cares."

Savy read it over my shoulder. "Sawyer?" she asked me.

A huge grin spread over my face. When I stood on tiptoe I could see over the huge amp at the side of the stage, and I saw Sawyer leaning against the wall. He looked so darling. I could just picture us together, a couple. We'd go to hear music together, and to the amusement park at Opryland. We'd write songs together, really great songs, which Sawyer's father would decide to record. No, *we'd* record them. And get a big record deal. And Sawyer would take me in his arms and tell me we were made for each other. He'd kiss me passionately, and my clothes would magically drop off of me without any fumbling, and then we'd—

"I told you he liked you," Savy said, giving

me a hug. "And you look totally darling tonight."

I snapped out of my fantasy. For once, reality wasn't so bad. "Thanks," I replied, floating on a sea of bliss. I looked down at myself in my fringed top that exposed my midriff, and I shook my flowing hair off my face.

I was ready to rock 'n' roll.

Impetuously I reached for a pen I saw lying on a nearby table, and I scribbled on the back of Sawyer's note: "You're pretty awesome yourself. See you after!"

"Excuse me," I said, tapping the volunteer who'd given me the note on her shoulder. "Do you think you could give this back to the guy who gave it to you?"

"Yeah, sure. I have to go back out to set up some extra chairs, anyway," the girl said, slipping the note into her pocket.

Wynonna finished her last number, and the crowd went wild. She waved and ran off the stage with her band.

The head of the Juvenile Arthritis Foundation came out and made a pitch for donations while behind her a bunch of guys quickly set up our instruments. I caught Gramma Beth's eye—she was standing on the other side of the stage—and she gave me the big thumbs-up sign.

All too soon the donation pitch was over, and Andi Jennings, the hot up-and-coming young country singer who was one of the MCs, was introducing us.

"This is a great new band worth keeping your eye on, folks," Andi said. "We're proud to bring you their debut performance tonight. Please put your hands together for Wild Hearts!"

Did I say I was ready to rock 'n' roll?

Correction.

I was ready to fall over in a dead faint.

But I didn't. I ran out on stage and picked up my guitar, slipping the strap around my neck. I looked over at my friends. This was it.

Savy counted us in, and we launched into our rocking version of "It Wasn't God Who Made Honky Tonk Angels." At first I was on automatic pilot. But about halfway through the song I realized nothing catastrophic was going to happen, and I started to kind of almost . . . enjoy it. Oh, I knew I was stiff, that I wasn't really letting loose, but I was out there and I was hitting the right notes. At least it was a start. Savy's voice soared on the lead, and we all came in on our harmony parts. The sound system was great, and I could hear how good we sounded through the monitors.

When we finished, the crowd applauded politely. Well, so far, so good. They hadn't booed us off the stage in comparison with Wynonna. They hadn't walked out.

But I knew—we all knew—we could do better.

"Thank you very much," Savy said into her mike. "This next tune was written by our drummer, Jane. It's called "Love Won't Wait.""

Savy led us into Jane's song. I could tell we were all feeling more confident now. Savy's voice soared on the vocal lines and we sounded strong and true on the harmonies.

Life's too short to hesitate,
So get down now, baby,
Cuz Love Won't Wait!

This was it, my first guitar solo. I closed my eyes and gave myself up to the music, bending the notes until they sounded like they were crying. I heard someone in the audience whoop when I pulled off my hottest lick, and then we all came back in on the final notes.

Love Won't Wait
Oh, no,
My Love Won't Wait!

This time the applause was louder, some people whistled, and I was grinning to beat the band. Savy jumped off the piano bench and ran over to me and Sandra. We were standing near enough to Jane so that she could hear, too.

"Let's kick ass!" she whispered to us fiercely.

She was right. Good wasn't good enough.

Savy ran back to the piano, spun around, and counted us off into the mike. We jumped into "Great Balls of Fire."

Yes, this was it! Now we were doing what we'd done in rehearsal. We rocked the place out! People were clapping, dancing in the aisles, yelling encouragement at us.

We all took solos. I burned up the guitar. And all the time I was thinking about Sawyer out there watching me, liking me, maybe even one day loving me.

"Goodness, gracious, Great Balls of Fire!"

I played the last guitar riff and then jumped high in the air to the beat of the very last note.

The place went wild.

We ran offstage and hugged each other, jumping up and down.

"That was Wild Hearts," Andi Jennings said into the mike. "Come on back out here and take a bow!"

The audience was still applauding and screaming. We ran out onstage and took a bow together, then ran off again. Gramma Beth and Savy's parents were there, waiting for us.

"Girls, you are fabulous!" Gramma Beth cried, hugging each and every one of us.

"It was so much fun!" I replied, tingling with happiness.

"Kimmy girl, you got the music in you," Savy's dad told me.

"I love it, I just love it!" I hugged myself hard. Everything was so great!

"There's a few more acts on the bill," Gramma Beth said. "Why don't ya'll find some seats out there, and then later we'll all go out and celebrate."

I didn't need any more prompting to go and find Sawyer.

I went around the long way, coming in from the back of the ballroom so I wouldn't disturb anyone. A mandolin player was up on stage, playing some mournful mountain music. I stood on tiptoe and looked around for Sawyer. I squinted—things were so blurry without my glasses—but finally I saw him, sitting on the far right aisle.

As unobtrusively as I could I tiptoed over to him. When he saw me, he grinned and got up. As we headed for the back door, he grabbed my hand and held it tight.

When we got out to the lobby, I turned to him.

He looked at me, admiration written across his face. "Kimmy, you were awesome," he said.

Exactly what he'd written to me in the note he'd sent backstage.

I was in love.

Slowly he raised his hand and touched my hair and moved closed, his lips heading for mine. I closed my eyes, breathlessly anticipating Sawyer Paxton's kiss.

But just before Sawyer's lips touched mine, I felt a tap on my shoulder.

I turned around. It was Dave Mallone.

"Hi, Kimmy," Dave said. His eyes narrowed and darted to Sawyer, then back to me.

"Dave," I said, trying to hide the fact that I was ready to kill him, "what are you doing here?"

"I came to see you, of course," Dave said, as if that made sense. Slowly he reached into his pocket and pulled out a folded piece of paper. A piece of paper From Someone Who Cares.

Not from Sawyer. From *him*.

Dave held up his note, his eyes glittering with love. He reached for my hand. "Thanks for writing back," he said. "Could you excuse us, Sawyer? Kimmy and I have a date."

CHAPTER
9

I pulled away from Dave.

"No, we don't have a date," I said in a low voice.

Dave blushed and he blinked rapidly. "Sure, we do," he insisted. He held up his note. "You said so right here."

Sawyer looked at me expectantly.

"Dave, I'm sorry," I began, "but I . . . I didn't know that note was from you."

Now all the color drained out of Dave's face. I felt so bad for him. Oh, in the back of my mind I knew it was crazy—I mean, I had never invited him to the show—but he was just so pathetic, so much like I *used* to be.

"Could you excuse us for just a second?" I asked Sawyer.

"Sure," he said easily, though I could tell by the look in his eye that he thought something was very, very strange.

I pulled Dave over to the corner of the room. He had on what looked like spanking new jeans and a nice forest green shirt with a string tie. He was trying so hard, it made my eyes hurt. And I ached for him. Because I knew just how he felt.

"Look, Dave, I appreciate your coming to see the band and everything—"

"Hey, I wouldn't have missed it for anything!" Dave said earnestly.

"Well, thanks," I replied. "How did you even know about it, anyway?"

"You told me about it," he said calmly.

I thought a moment. "No, I didn't."

"Yes, you did," Dave insisted. "In school. A few days ago."

I racked my brain, but I couldn't remember. Still, maybe I *had* told him. Everyone at school had been talking about it. And things had been so hectic lately that it was certainly possible I had just forgotten.

"Look, Dave, I'm glad you came, but—"

"You are?" he interrupted hopefully.

"Yes, we're friends," I said. "But ... I'm sorry, I have a date with Sawyer."

Dave's mouth twitched. He blinked rapidly. "Oh, okay," he finally said.

"I really am glad you came," I said again. I just couldn't help myself.

"Oh, yeah, well, you know . . ." he muttered, backing away from me. "I'll see ya." He took off rapidly across the lobby.

"What was that all about?" Sawyer asked me when I walked back over to him.

"I don't know," I sighed. "I think maybe he has a crush on me or something."

Sawyer reached for my hand. "Hey, I can understand that."

I smiled shyly. His hand felt so good. He was so gorgeous.

"Listen," Sawyer continued, "ya'll are great. I really mean it. You are mega-talented, Kimmy."

"You think?"

"I know," Sawyer insisted. "If you weren't already in a band I'd try to talk you into starting one with me."

Sawyer took a step toward me and leaned close. There was hardly anyone around. Everyone was still inside listening to the music. "Where was I before?" he asked me in a low voice. Then his hand reached for my cheek. He touched me oh-so-gently, drawing me close.

And then Sawyer Paxton, the boy I'd had a crush on forever, kissed me.

"Wow," I breathed softly as he pulled away.

"Wow as in good?" he asked, a twinkle in his eye.

"Wow as in wow," was all I could manage.

He laughed and enveloped me in a huge hug.

"Oh, Kimmy, there you are!" Savy cried, running over to us. "Hey, Sawyer."

"Hey. Listen, ya'll were just great," Sawyer told Savy. He draped his arm casually around my shoulders.

"Thanks," Savy replied, "Maybe you'll write us a song sometime."

"I might could do that," Sawyer said. "I had no idea you had such a great voice."

"She's better than Trisha Yearwood, I think," I told Sawyer.

"Well, you're biased," Savy replied. "Listen, my gramma and my parents want to take us all out to celebrate. Sandra and Jane are backstage with them. Ya'll want to come?"

As much as I love Savy's family, I was hoping Sawyer would say no.

And he did.

"Gee, if Kimmy doesn't mind, I was hoping to take her over to this session on Music Row where Great Plains is recording. They're friends of mine. But if you'd rather go with Savy—"

"Oh, no, that's fine," I said quickly.

"Well, then, I'll call you tomorrow," Savy said, giving me a quick hug. "Have fun!"

Sawyer turned to me. "You heard the lady. Let's go have fun!"

"I just have to go backstage and get my guitar," I told Sawyer.

We quickly walked backstage and found my guitar, then went out to Sawyer's car. As he pulled out of the parking lot, I noticed someone in a red Toyota pull out behind us.

And I thought it looked like Dave.

But, no, that was crazy. There was no way that Dave had waited for me.

There was a lot of traffic when we pulled on to Briley Parkway, and I craned my neck to see if the red Toyota was behind us.

It wasn't. So I had only been imagining things.

I looked over at Sawyer and smiled. He smiled back. Suddenly I felt shy again. I just couldn't believe I was out with Sawyer, that he'd kissed me, that he really liked me, when I'd been so convinced that he didn't even know I was alive. Or worse, that he looked at me the same way I looked at Dave.

Then, as if he'd been reading my mind, Sawyer spoke up.

"You know, you're always so quiet in school, I was one surprised guy when I heard you wail on that guitar at the school play."

"I was scared to play in front of people," I confessed. "That was the very first time."

"No kidding?" Sawyer marveled. His eye flicked over me, but not in an obnoxious way. "You look different, too."

"You probably didn't even know I existed before," I blurted out, then regretted it instantly.

"Not true," Sawyer said. He changed lanes and took the I-40 exit to Music Row. "I always thought you were beautiful. But you seemed like you didn't think you were beautiful. Or you didn't want to be beautiful. Or something. And I always used to wonder about that."

"I always thought you were beautiful, too," I confessed in a low voice.

"Well, dang, I'm not!" Sawyer insisted. He managed a quick look at me, then turned his eyes back to the road. "Did you really?"

I nodded.

"Well, you could knock me over with a feather," Sawyer marveled.

"But ... you mean you don't think you're good-looking?" I asked him.

"Not hardly," he snorted. "Now, my older brother, Casey, he's the good-looking one. He went to New York to be a model."

"But you're so confident," I marveled. "I mean, you played Danny in *Grease*. You had to be cute and sexy." I blushed at what I'd said.

"Oh, shoot, that's just acting," Sawyer said. "That's why I like it. I get to pretend to be things I'm not." He pulled into a parking space in front of Wall of Sound Studios on Twenty-first Avenue and turned to me. He took my hand in his. "Fact is, Kimmy, I'm pretty shy my own damn self. It's scary to let people really know you, don't you think?"

I smiled at him. At that moment I would have danced naked down Twenty-first Avenue if he'd asked me to.

Fortunately he didn't, and we got out of the car and walked toward the studio hand in hand.

And even though I was in a state of near-perfect bliss, somewhere though the haze I registered this fact: a red Toyota had just pulled in across the street.

"Wait, you're telling me you think that Dave Mallone followed you to the recording session with Sawyer?" Jane asked me.

It was the next night, and we were all over at Savy's doing a postmortem on our first gig. We all agreed that although we'd taken a while to get into it, in the end it had gone really well. Gramma Beth said that the fund-raising organizers had told her how terrific they thought we were. When we took a break from band business, I told Sandra, Savy, and Jane about my date with Sawyer, and the thing with Dave came up.

"Well, I'm not sure," I hedged. "I mean, I didn't actually *see* Dave there. There are a lot of red Toyotas out there. I grabbed one of Gramma Beth's homemade cookies and nibbled around the edges nervously.

"Listen, this guy is a major wanker," Jane insisted. "I'm telling you, he's the one who's been making the bizarro phone calls to you."

"Are you still getting them?" Sandra asked me, frowning.

"Yeah," I confessed. "But the person never says anything."

"It's Dave the Weenie!" Jane insisted.

"He's not a wanker," I shot back. For some weird reason I felt the need to defend him.

"Kimmy, you have to admit he's a strange guy," Savy said gently.

"Maybe you could encourage him to get help," Sandra suggested, polishing off a cookie.

"But I don't even know it's him making the phone calls," I pointed out. "Besides, he's harmless."

"How do you know?" Jane asked me.

"This isn't New York, Jane," I said. "Every guy is not a criminal."

"See, this is how New York gets a bad rap," Jane replied. "Only every *other* guy is a criminal."

"You care about Dave, am I right?" Sandra asked me.

I nodded. "I don't know why. I don't even like him, really, but I feel so sorry for him."

"Pity for a guy is *so* unattractive," Jane stated, twirling her drumsticks in the air.

"Here's my suggestion," Sandra continued, ignoring Jane. "Call him up and talk to him about all of this. If you're really his friend, that's what you'll do. Otherwise it's just lip service, just something to stroke your ego because he has this big crush on you."

"I'm not—" I protested, hurt by her remark.

Sandra shrugged. "It's your call."

"Hey, Sandra, phone for you," Savy's little sister, Shelly, called from the doorway.

"Use that one," Savy said, pointing to the princess phone next to the dilapidated aqua couch.

"Hello?" Sandra said into the phone. "Oh,

hi, Pete. Uh-huh. . . . Uh-huh. . . . Well, I'll ask them. . . . Okay. Bye." She turned to us. "That was Pete Gambol."

My eyebrows shot straight up. "You're going out with Pete Gambol?" Pete Gambol is a red-headed jock with a loud laugh who intimidates me to death.

"No, I am not going out with Pete Gambol," Sandra replied, giving me a withering look. "He's vice president of the junior class and I'm president, remember?"

"Oh, right," I muttered, blushing. Actually, I had forgotten all about it.

"Well, here's the deal," Sandra said briskly. "Pete is in charge of the entertainment for the junior class Autumn Fling."

"Get me the barf bag," Jane exclaimed. "Who invents these things?"

"It's just a dance," Savy replied. "It's been called the junior class Autumn Fling since my parents went to Green Hills High."

"I didn't know your parents went to Green Hills High," Jane said with surprise.

"That's where they met," Savy told her.

"No kidding?" Jane marveled. "So were they, like, in the same classes or—"

"Excuse me, but can we stick to the subject at hand?" Sandra asked, folding her arms and shooting Jane a look.

"Be my guest," Jane allowed.

"Pete called because Wyatt's band was supposed to play for the dance, but Wyatt can't play because of his broken arm—" Sandra began.

"I'd like to break his face," Jane put in.

"So Pete went to check out this other band tonight—from Hillsboro High. He said he heard they cooked, but they sucked. So some people who heard us play last night told him we were killer, and now he wants to know do we want to play for the dance?"

The room was quiet.

"Us?" I finally said. "Wild Hearts?"

"Too cool!" Savy exclaimed, jumping up to hug Sandra. "Tell him yes, yes, yes!"

"Hey, wait, are we ready for that?" Jane asked. "This is not a fund-raiser where we won't know anybody, you know."

"Come on, it's just a school dance," Savy wheedled. "And we're better than Thunder Rolls anyway."

"Let's vote," Sandra said. "Because I told him I'd call him back. In case it's slipped your mind, the Autumn Fling is next Saturday night."

"Wait! Hold the phone," Jane objected. "We're not talking a three-tune set here.

We're talking, what, three forty-five-minute sets? No way!"

"Just two sets," Sandra said. "The seniors put on a show for the juniors. It's a tradition."

"So, two forty-five minute sets," Jane amended. "I'm not going up there at Hocum High in front of the pastel people in their fall finery unless we are awesome, incredible, and unbelievable. End of report."

Savy touched Jane's arm. "Jane, you're not going to look stupid. We're really good. No one is going to make fun of you."

"Sha, right," Jane snorted. "Listen, I gotta vote no on this one."

"The pay is four hundred dollars," Sandra said quietly.

"Pay?" I squeaked. For some reason, that had never occurred to me.

"That's a hundred bucks each," Jane said. "I have to slave for twenty hours at Uncle Zap's to make that much money."

"Does that mean you change your vote?" Savy asked hopefully.

"Depends," Jane said. "Are we going to spend every possible moment between now and then practicing?"

"I've got a tennis match tomorrow afternoon," Sandra said. "And a junior class meeting Tuesday after school. Other than that I'm cool."

"I'm free," I said with a shrug. "I guess that doesn't surprise anyone."

"I've got some club meetings, but I'll skip them," Savy promised. "So, are we in?" She looked hopefully around the room. It was pretty clear Jane was the only holdout. Savy put her hands together in a praying gesture.

"Oh, great, this is just like how my family votes on things," Jane groused. "Oh, okay, yes, I'm in."

"Oh, God, I'm so excited!" Savy yelled, jumping up and down. "It's going to be too cool!"

"How about if we practice right now?" Jane said, slipping back behind the drums.

"You betcha!" Savy agreed, taking a run for her piano bench. She ran a finger down our list of A-tunes. "How about 'Twentieth Century Fox'?"

Jane smiled. This was an old Doors tune that we all loved. It was really far from country, and we all knew Savy was suggesting it to placate Jane, the country-music hater.

Even as we launched into the song, my mind was on Sawyer. Would he ever ask me out? Would he ignore me in school and pretend the whole evening we'd spent together had never happened? Everything had been so great at the recording studio. And afterward we'd gone out to eat; then he'd taken me home and kissed me on my mother's front porch. He'd left, saying a casual "See ya." Well, what did "See ya" mean, exactly?

It clearly didn't mean "Do you want to go with me to the junior class Autumn Fling," because he hadn't invited me. But now I was going to be there anyway, playing with the band. Maybe he just wasn't going.

Or maybe he *was* going. With someone else.

CHAPTER
10

Some people dream at night. Not me. I dream during the day. At night I obsess. Sunday night, for example, I obsessed about Sawyer. I liked him so much. And he seemed to like me. But if he really liked me why hadn't he asked me out? And who was he going to the Autumn Fling with? And how could I manage to wipe whoever that girl was off the face of the earth without getting a really big prison sentence?

The fact that my phone rang maybe twenty times with calls from my friendly neighborhood breather didn't help, either.

Once I snatched up the phone and said, "Is that you, Dave?" But all the person on the other end did was breathe.

So I tried to put the breather out of my mind, which took me back to obsessing about Sawyer.

Did he like me or didn't he? Yes or no? Over and over and over until I saw the sunlight creeping in through the window.

So that was when I finally came up with my plan. If I was going to get Sawyer, I had to look cute. Really cute. Well, maybe that wasn't possible, but I had to at least look cuter than the washed-out thing that I usually looked like. I know Sawyer had said he'd always thought I was beautiful, but the more I thought about that, the more I was sure he was lying to be nice.

I'd have to take a chance. But Sawyer was worth it.

I got up and showered, then blew my hair dry from underneath so it would get as pouffy as possible. Then I rummaged through my clothes. I've already told you what my wardrobe looks like, and I wasn't about to wear Savy's lace cat suit to school, but I did find a plain white T-shirt of my dad's and I laid that out on my bed. Then I looked through my skirts. All long, all baggy. Impetuously I grabbed a long denim skirt and took a pair of sharp scissors out of my desk. I cut the skirt off short. Really short. Then I slipped on the

T-shirt and my newly frayed-bottom denim miniskirt. Next I got out my bag of cosmetics and put on some eyeliner, mascara, and lipstick. It was tricky because I had to keep slipping my glasses back on to get it right—I vowed to try contact lenses again. I had a little sample of perfume that the saleslady had given me when I bought the makeup, and I put some of that on my pulse points. I turned to the mirror to survey the finished product.

A thin, cute blond looked back at me. Her shoulders were kind of hunched over, like she didn't believe she was worth looking at. So I straightened my shoulders. And tossed my hair. And practiced various looks in the mirror.

The Oh-hi-Sawyer-it's-nice-to-see-you-but-I'm-too-cool-to-really-care-all-that-much smile.

The Oh-really-you-want-to-take-me-to-the-school-dance-well-let-me-check-my-datebook raised eyebrow.

The phone rang.

"Hello?"

The breather.

I breathed back ostentatiously and hung up.

Then I grabbed up my purse and my courage and headed downstairs to face my mother.

She looked up from her perfectly poached egg. "*What* are you wearing?" she asked slowly.

"Clothes," I said, attempting a nonchalant tone. It was Mrs. Gruller's day off, so I poured myself a cup of tea and reached for one of the carrot muffins Mrs. Gruller had made the day before.

"Yes, Kimberly, I can see that they might be loosely referred to as clothes, though clearly they are inappropriate clothes. Am I correct?"

"That is a subjective opinion," I replied carefully, cutting the muffin in two.

"Yes, and as I am the nonsubjective head of this household, I believe I have a say in what my daughter wears to school." Mother blotted her lips with her linen napkin and laid it carefully on her lap. She waited.

"I'm old enough to decide what I want to wear," I said.

"And what you want to wear is your father's T-shirt and a short denim rag?" she bit off.

"I like it," I replied evenly.

Mother sipped her tea deliberately. Then she put her cup down. Then she opened her mouth. "Kimberly, are you having sex?"

I was shocked to the roots of my hair. I blushed a furious red. "Am I *what?*"

"I asked if you were having sex," my mother repeated.

"What kind of a question is that?" I shrieked. "How can you ask me that?"

"You have started dressing like some kind of little tramp, so I am asking you if, in fact, you are acting the way you are dressing."

I jumped up from the table. "Yes, Mother," I replied furiously. "I am sleeping with every boy in my class. Simultaneously."

"Don't you speak that way to me, Kimberly—"

"I don't want to speak to you at all," I interrupted, tears coming to my eyes. "Why can't you just . . . just leave me alone? God!"

"Don't take the Lord's name in vain in this house."

"I don't even want to *be* in this house! I—"

"I suppose you get this from Savy. I suppose it's my own fault for letting you associate with those people."

"I love *those* people!" I cried. "*Those* people have more love in their little finger than you've ever shown me in my whole life!"

I saw the hurt hit my mother's face like a slap. "How can you say that?" she asked in a soft, injured voice.

I closed my eyes. This was so awful. And I hadn't slept at all. I just wanted to crawl back under my blankets—not try, not take any chances. Why did everything always have to be so hard and scary?

But I couldn't share any of that with my

mother. So instead of saying anything at all I just picked up my schoolbooks and headed out the door where the chauffeur who worked on Mr. Gruller's day off was waiting for me.

"Kimmy? Woa, you look fantastic!" Savy shrieked when she saw me in the hall before our first class. She gave me a huge hug.

"Really?" I asked. I was already feeling better, just hearing her vote of support.

"This is so cool!" Savy cried, twirling me around. "I'm so proud of you!"

A group of kids walked by. I saw them all check me out with looks of surprise on their faces.

"I feel so self-conscious," I confessed in a whisper. "It's like I'm naked or something!"

"Kimmy!" Jane strode over to us. "Yeah, now you look like you play lead guitar for Wild Hearts! Get down!"

Wyatt Shane and his friend Billy walked by. I saw Wyatt's eyebrows go up as he took in my long legs.

"Is the skirt too short?" I asked my friends, tugging it down self-consciously.

"No way," Savy assured me.

"So, listen," Jane said, "I messed up my schedule at Uncle Zap's, and I'm supposed to work tonight."

"But we've got band practice!" Savy protested.

"I know, I'm gonna call in at lunch and see if I can switch with someone, but the store manager has the IQ of a turnip and—"

"I'm glad I ran into you guys," Sandra said, hurrying over to us. "I've got a huge hassle tonight. My tennis coach says I have to hit with this girl. I've been missing practice, and he's ticked off at me, so—"

"Hold it!" Savy yelled, holding up her hand. "I thought we were going to make a commitment to the band this week so we could play for the dance? What is all this?"

"You think I *want* to slave at Uncle Zap's?" Jane asked. "The job seriously sucks, but—"

"Hi, girls." It was Wyatt Shane and his idiot friend Billy. Smirking.

"Go crawl back under your rock," Jane spat at him.

"As long as you don't crawl under there with me, scag-meat," Wyatt replied easily. Billy laughed.

Jane took a menacing step toward Wyatt, but Sandra put a restraining hand on Jane's arm. "Chill," Sandra advised her in a low voice.

"We're busy here," Savy told Wyatt.

"In other words, go away," Sandra added.

Wyatt shrugged and sauntered around my three friends until he stood right by me. "You want me to go away too, pretty Kimmy?"

"Yes," I managed.

Wyatt slowly looked me all the way down and back up again until I wished I had on my usual baggy clothes. "That's too bad," he finally said. "Because I kind of thought you dressed like that so I'd notice you."

"I don't dress for you," I told him. He was so icky. I couldn't believe I had ever thought he was cute.

"Okay, how about *un*dressing for me, then," he suggested. He looked over at Billy, who guffawed as if Wyatt had said something really swift.

"How about just leaving me alone?" I knew it was a lame comeback, but I'm not like Jane, who can devastate people with her witty comebacks.

"For now," Wyatt said insolently. "But I'll be catching you later." Then he and Billy swaggered away.

"Please, tell me I never actually went out with him," Jane moaned.

"It was temporary insanity," Savy assured her.

The bell rang for first period.

"Shoot, we haven't settled any of this!" Savy fumed.

"At lunch," Sandra promised and hurried off to first period.

I headed for my first class and suddenly found Dave Mallone heading down the hall with me.

"You look beautiful," he said reverently.

"Thanks, Dave," I said. I tried to walk with enough space between us so that no one would think we were together. Then I felt guilty and moved over. As we walked down the hall, I looked for Sawyer, but I didn't see him. Everyone else was around, though. Staring at me, mouths agape.

"See ya," I said to Dave when I got to my classroom door.

Dave leaned over and kissed my cheek before I could stop him. And at that exact moment I saw Sawyer across the hall, looking at me and Dave.

"Stop that!" I yelled at Dave, jumping away from him.

"Oh, sorry, I just thought . . ." Dave's hands flew around with anxiety. He couldn't even finish his sentence.

I saw Sawyer disappear into a classroom. I knew he'd seen me and Dave.

"You've got to cut this stuff out, Dave," I

insisted, sounding angry and flustered because of Sawyer.

"But, Kimmy, I love you," Dave whispered intensely.

"You don't even know me!" I yelled, and, turning on my heel, I left Dave standing there and marched into my class.

By lunchtime I was miserable. I felt as if everyone in the whole school was talking about me, pointing at me. *Did you see the way Kimmy is dressed? Did you hear that she and Dave the Weenie Mallone are a major item?* And worst of all, Sawyer Paxton didn't notice me at all. It was like I didn't exist.

So. That was what I got for trying too hard.

I got a glass of juice and sat down with Savy and Sandra, who were trying to figure out a band practice schedule. I was so depressed and so sick of looking at everything through a blur that I put my glasses back on.

"Why can't you hit tennis balls with this girl next week, after the school dance?" Savy was asking Sandra.

"I have a commitment to the tennis team—" Sandra began.

"Well, you have a commitment to us, too," Savy argued.

"I know that," Sandra replied, stirring the

fruit up from the bottom of her carton of yogurt. "I'm doing the best I can with my limited resources."

"Okay, you guys, I got out of work tonight," Jane announced, hurrying over to our table. She was dressed in a Christmas motif, with green leggings and a long sweatshirt covered with Christmas trees. A tiny piece of tinsel held back one side of her hair.

Jane plopped down next to Savy and grabbed a potato chip off her tray. "I had to seriously eat dirt for that idiot manager—like I had to promise to baby-sit for his two-year-old rug rat next week—but I did it."

Sandra got up. "I'll go talk to the tennis coach," she said with a sigh.

"Thanks, I love you," Savy cried.

"Yeah, well, my coach hates me right about now, so I'll take all the love I can get," Sandra replied. "Later."

"What is the biggie?" Jane asked, grabbing another chip from Savy. "How can she even compare tennis to music? Who cares about hitting a little ball over a net?"

"A few million people," Savy said, polishing off her turkey sandwich. She looked over at me. "You're awfully quiet, even for you."

I shrugged and stared morosely at my orange juice.

"You okay?" Savy asked. "You're wearing your glasses again, I noticed."

I shrugged again. "I hate my life."

"But you look so darling today," Savy protested. "Even with your glasses. And everything is going so great—".

"Sawyer Paxton does not know I'm alive," I replied glumly.

"But he kissed you," Savy reminded me.

"That was then, this is now," I said with a sigh. "I was so stupid to think it meant anything."

"Hey, I saw the two of you together," Jane said, fiddling with the Christmas tree lights that adorned her wrist. "The guy definitely likes you."

"Yeah, I guess that's why he ignored me all morning," I said morosely. "Now I just look like a total fool, wearing this little skirt and this makeup as if I thought he could like me when of course he couldn't like me and he doesn't like me and he never will like me."

Jane and Savy just stared at me.

"That's the most I ever heard you say at one time," Jane marveled.

"Quack-quack," two of the pastel people honked at Jane as they sashayed by our table. It was Katie Lynn Kilroy and her friend, Muffy

Sorbette. They were dressed in their cheer-leader outfits and looked extremely cute.

I looked over at Jane to see how she was taking it. She just crunched away on Savy's potato chips like she could care less.

"You know what I heard?" Katie Lynn said to Muffy in a loud voice. "I heard that she doesn't even have any panties on under that funny-looking sawed-off skirt!"

Poor Jane. How could she stand it?

But wait a second. Jane wasn't wearing a skirt.

I was.

"Well, the thing has been slowly unraveling all morning," Muffy said. "I figure by fifth period she'll just be standing around completely starkers!"

Oh, my God, they were talking about me.

"Ignore them," Jane advised me.

"They're morons," Savy added.

"Is my skirt really unraveling?" I whispered to my friends, completely mortified. I reached down under the table to feel the bottom of my skirt. Maybe you couldn't just cut off denim without it fraying so much that soon you weren't wearing anything at all.

"It's fine, Kimmy," Savy assured me. "Honest."

When Katie Lynn and Muffy saw me frantically feeling the bottom of my skirt they laughed hysterically, falling over each other. Then they ran over to a group of their friends to share their mirth.

Savy and Jane tried to make me feel better, but nothing helped. I put my head down on the table and wished that I could crawl into a hole and stay there forever.

Just like some terrible nightmare, the day crawled along in slow motion. But finally the bell rang for my last class, and I headed toward the front door. I was supposed to meet Jane, Savy, and Sandra at Sandra's Jeep. I kept feeling for the bottom of my skirt. Every time a thread came off, I was sure the whole thing was falling apart. Just as I rounded the corner to the front hall of school I saw Dave Mallone. I turned away as if I hadn't seen him and hurried to the door.

"Kimmy!"

That voice did not belong to Dave Mallone. I would have recognized that voice anywhere. I turned around.

It was Sawyer.

He caught up with me.

"Listen, I just wanted to say hi."

"Hi," I said, staring at the floor.

He just stood there.

Finally I looked up. "Is that it?"

"No, I ..." He ran his hand through his hair nervously.

I was certain that he wanted to tell me about his real girlfriend, the one he was taking to the school dance that he had forgotten to mention to me. I waited for the inevitable.

"Look, I was kind of avoiding you today," he admitted in a low voice.

"You don't owe me anything," I managed. "I mean, it's okay. I know you must have a girlfriend. Which, like I said, is fine, because—"

"Because you're going out with Dave Mallone?" Sawyer asked me.

"No!" I replied quickly. "No, I'm not! Not at all!"

"But I thought—"

"How could you think that?" I broke in. "I mean, why would you—"

"Because Dave told me ya'll were, like, a serious item," Sawyer explained.

I was going to kill Dave Mallone with my bare hands.

"It's not true," I insisted. "And don't you remember I told you that he just has a crush on me?"

"Yeah, you did," Sawyer agreed. His hand

went sailing through his hair again. "I'm sorry, Kimmy. I'm not real good at this."

Good at what? Telling a girl who was in love with him that he didn't give a rat's ass about her? How come I'd never understood what he meant?

"Look, you don't have to say anything," I finally managed. "I have to go." I turned toward the door.

"Wait!" Sawyer said, touching my arm. I waited. "This isn't coming out how I wanted it to come out. What I wanted to say is that, well, I've been thinking about you. A lot."

You could have knocked me over with a feather.

"You have?" I squeaked.

Sawyer nodded. "But my brother, Casey— he's the one I told you about who went to New York to be a model—well, he just got arrested for drug possession—it's all a big mess—and it's gonna end up in the newspapers on account of my dad being who he is—"

"Famous," I added helpfully.

"Yeah, at least in this town," Sawyer explained. "I'm really worried about Casey, and it's kind of messing me up. I'm trying to figure if I should try to get to New York, you know, to see if I could help him. . . ."

Sawyer looked so sad, and I was so happy

to know that he hadn't really been ignoring me that I found the nerve to put my hand in his. He smiled at me gratefully.

"Anyway, I'm just real sorry to lay this all on you."

"It's okay," I assured him, squeezing his hand.

He smiled at me. "You're terrific, Kimmy. I mean it. So listen, I was wondering. I'm in this songwriters' group. We meet once a month, and we're meeting this Wednesday at my house. Everyone in the group is young—high school and college age, mostly—but a few of the members have already had songs recorded. I was thinking that if ya'll are free, you might could play a few tunes for the group."

"You mean Wild Hearts?"

"Right. I think they'd be so blown away that ya'll would end up getting a lot of demo work."

"We're playing for the school dance Saturday," I told Sawyer, even though what Wild Hearts was doing on Saturday didn't have anything to do with what we would or wouldn't do on Wednesday.

But I just couldn't help myself. My heart pounded in my chest. I had to know. Who was he going to the dance with?

"Is there a school dance Saturday?" Sawyer

asked with surprise. "Huh. I never keep track of that stuff. I guess I have my head buried in my music so much that I forget what's going on in the world."

Now I grinned hugely. He wasn't going with anyone else! He wasn't going at all!

"I'll ask the rest of the band about Wednesday," I told Sawyer.

"Great," Sawyer replied. He shuffled nervously for a second. "I, uh . . . well, I'd like to come to that dance and hear you play Saturday," he finally said. "And maybe we could go out after?"

Yes! Yes! Yes! Yes!

"That would be nice," I said casually, resisting the urge to jump up and down screaming like a fool.

"Thanks for being so understanding," Sawyer said, giving me a quick hug. "Hey, I forgot to tell you how fine you're looking today," he added.

"I am?" I asked, blushing happily.

"For real," Sawyer assured me. "I should have told you sooner, but when I have a problem and I get to brooding, I just shut everyone out sometimes."

I kissed his cheek quickly. "Thanks for telling me," I whispered, and then I turned and ran for the door.

I flew down the front steps and headed for the parking lot as if someone had put wings on my shoes.

"Looking for me?"

It was Wyatt Shane, leaning against a tree, smoking a cigarette.

"No," I said and started to hurry past him.

"Hey, hey, just a second," Wyatt said, stepping into my path.

"What?" I asked him. "I'm late."

"I just wanted to tell you how hot you look."

"Thanks." I took a step around him.

He stepped in my way again.

"Your legs are unbelievable, Kimmy," Wyatt continued in his sexy, low voice. He took a last drag on his cigarette and then stomped it out.

"Yeah, unbelievable," his friend Billy echoed, walking over to stand next to Wyatt.

Wyatt reached out to touch my hair. "You and I should get together sometime."

"I don't want to get together with you," I told him.

He put his hand to his heart as if I'd injured him, but his little grin said that he was too self-confident to really be injured by anything.

"Feel what you do to me," he said, and he took my hand and put it over his heart.

"Look, I'm late to meet my friends," I told him, snatching back my hand.

"Okay, give me one kiss and you can go," Wyatt said playfully.

"I don't want to kiss you," I said, trying to step around him again.

He blocked me again, his sidekick Billy with him. "Come on, shy little Kimmy. You know you want to." He reached for my arm with his left hand—the one that wasn't in a cast. I pulled away.

"Leave her alone."

I looked behind me. It was Dave Mallone, coming to my rescue.

"Oh, this is rich," Wyatt said, cracking up. "Weenie Mallone is coming to the rescue!" Wyatt laughed even harder, and Billy joined in, cackling like a hyena. Kids began to turn and watch us with interest, a dozen near the school steps, a few on the lawn near the parking lot.

"Hey, Kimmy, move it!" Sandra called, heading toward us from the parking lot with Savy and Jane. She stomped across the grass angrily. "What is your problem?"

"Come on, sweet Kimmy," Wyatt urged, ignoring everyone and reaching for me again. He obviously enjoyed being the center of attention. "Just pay your toll and you can go by."

"I told you to leave her alone and I meant it," Dave said. He took a quick step toward Wyatt and pulled his fist back, ready to make contact with Wyatt's face, but Wyatt was quicker, and even throwing a left-handed punch, he made sickening contact with Dave's nose before Dave could touch him. I heard a crunching sound, and blood spurted out of Dave's nose.

"Don't mess with me, little boy," Wyatt told Dave menacingly. I heard some people behind me titter.

My friends were running toward me, Dave Mallone was bleeding all over the place, kids were shrieking and pointing at us, and still Wyatt reached for me again.

At that moment something in me snapped. I got so angry that I forgot to be scared. Just as he came toward me I remembered what Nancy Larsen had taught us in the self-defense seminar. I lifted my knee and made sharp contact with Wyatt's groin.

"Aghhhh!" Wyatt screamed, and doubled over in agony.

"Now you can really go crawl back under your rock," Jane told him, reaching us at just that instant. "Are you okay?" she asked me.

I nodded and turned to Dave. "Can we take

you to the hospital or something, Dave?" I asked him.

He held his nose, blood seeping between his fingers, down over his ugly print shirt, and onto his too-new jeans.

"Just leave me alone," he sobbed, pulling away from me.

"But—"

"Haven't you humiliated me enough?" he screamed at me, and then before I could say or do anything, Dave Mallone ran away from all of us as fast as he could.

CHAPTER
11

$\heartsuit$

*M*aybe I should have run after him, but I didn't.

I'm not proud of that.

I let Dave go, and rationalized that he really didn't want me hovering over him.

In fact, I forgot about Dave because I was so busy thinking about Sawyer. That he really did like me. That he'd invited the band to play for his group on Wednesday. That he wanted to come to the dance with me. Dave Mallone and his bloody nose just flew right out of my head.

I'm not proud of that, either.

At band practice we all voted to play at Sawyer's house on Wednesday—one of the few times we've all agreed about anything—but we all could see the value of playing for a small group just three days before our big debut at the school dance.

We practiced like crazy on Monday and Tuesday. I stayed at my dad's house so I wouldn't have to deal with my mother, and I wore some of my own clothes mixed with some of Savy's. Not really wild—I would never live down the cutoff denim skirt nightmare—but not so conservative, either. And I wore makeup. And perfume. Sawyer paid attention to me in school, seeking me out, walking me to my classes, and he even called me Tuesday evening.

As for Dave, he wasn't in school. Not on Monday, Tuesday, or Wednesday.

And the breather stopped calling me.

Wyatt wasn't in school either. I was glad about that.

I told all this to Jane, Savy, and Sandra on the way to Sawyer's house Wednesday night. We were in Sandra's Jeep. The windows were open and the tape deck was cranking out Garth Brooks's latest CD. I had to yell over the music.

"So there's your proof," Jane yelled back at me, pushing her windblown hair out of her face. "Dave is the breather."

"Or Wyatt," Savy pointed out. "He wasn't in school either."

"Wyatt isn't that subtle," Jane yelled over the music. "If he wanted to harass you he'd send you a horse's head in the mail or something."

"Oh, listen to this, you guys," Sandra called to us, cranking the music up as Garth began singing his next tune. "My mom sings all the backup solos on this one!"

We dutifully listened to Sandra's mom singing, and she was great, but I was thinking about Dave. I turned around to reach under me on the seat—a pencil or something was sticking into me—and that was when I saw a red car behind us that looked just like Dave's.

But that was ridiculous. I was just feeling guilty.

When the song ended, so did that side of the tape, and I was thankful for the quiet. I really wanted to talk to my friends.

"Listen, do ya'll think I should . . . call Dave or something?" I asked them.

"Get a grip, Kimmy!" Jane exclaimed. "You only just got the guy to stop calling you!"

"Yeah, but he hasn't been in school since Wyatt broke his nose."

"Maybe he just doesn't want to come to

school with his face all black-and-blue," Savy pointed out.

"Yeah, I'm sure that's it," Sandra agreed. "I mean, the kid takes enough ragging at school. It's no wonder he doesn't want to show up with his nose and eyes all purple-looking. That'd be like begging for more abuse."

"I suppose," I sighed, chewing nervously on a strand of my hair.

"Call him if it'll make you feel better," Savy said to me in a low voice, giving my hand a squeeze.

I smiled at her gratefully. Savy is the greatest friend in the entire world.

When we got to Sawyer's house, there were about twenty-five people in the little rehearsal studio, which just about filled it to capacity. We wedged our way in, and Sawyer worked his way through the noisy crowd to greet us.

"Hey," he greeted me, kissing my cheek. "Ya'll look great."

We had decided to wear jeans or shorts and T-shirts—very casual—and save our stage out-fits for the dance on Saturday. I had on a pair of jeans I'd found at the mall the day before, on a very quick trip with Savy before band practice, and a Jim Morrison T-shirt I bought because I wanted to impress Jane.

"Big crowd," I commented nervously. "I . . .

I didn't know there would be so many people here." Fear crept up my spine like a daddy longlegs.

"They're gonna love you," Sawyer assured me, giving me a little hug.

"What did you do, sell tickets?" Jane asked, as two more people pushed their way into the studio.

"I just put the word out that ya'll were definitely worth a listen," Sawyer said.

"And everyone knows you have great taste, is that it?" Sandra asked, looking amused.

"There's also free food," Sawyer admitted with a laugh. "My dad springs for a buffet afterward, back at the house."

"Aha! Everyone's here for the food!" Savy laughed.

"What can I tell you, there are a lot of starving musicians in this town," Sawyer said. "So, you ladies ready to play?"

"Now?" I screeched, biting my lip with consternation.

"You don't need to be nervous," Sawyer assured me.

"Oh, yes, I do," I insisted, gulping hard.

"She goes through this every time we play," Sandra explained to Sawyer.

"All I can think is why do I put myself through this?" I wondered out loud, wringing my hands. "No one is forcing me to get up and play the guitar in public, so—"

"Wrong," Jane interrupted. "*You're* forcing you."

"Oh, well, I never listen to me," I quipped nervously, wiping my sweaty palms off on my jeans.

"Hey, Kimmy made a joke!" Sandra exclaimed. Then she gave me a quick poke in the ribs. "I'm teasing you."

"Oh, I know," I assured her. "I'm okay. Really. I'm fine. Completely. Uh, where's the bathroom?"

Sawyer pointed to the other side of the studio, and I worked my way through the crowd until I reached the bathroom. I shut the door and leaned against it, the muffled sounds of all those voices coming at me from the other side of the door.

I looked into the mirror. A ghostly pale face looked back at me. "You can do this," I told my reflection. Then I did all the usual bathroom stuff, gave myself another pep talk in the mirror, and headed back into the studio.

Savy, Sandra, and Jane were all standing near the instruments in the corner of the room. I wove my way through the bodies until I reached them. More people had evidently arrived while I was in the john—I looked out at a sea of expectant faces.

"Your lucky guitar," Sawyer told me with a grin, handing me his dad's guitar that Elvis had played. I took it gratefully and looped the strap around my neck. Sandra strapped on her bass, Savy took a seat at the piano, and Jane went behind the drums.

"Okay, listen up!" Sawyer called to the crowd. "I guess most of you heard through the grapevine that my friends would be playing a few tunes tonight—"

"What we heard about was the free food!" a guy in the crowd yelled out.

There was good-natured laughter from the crowd.

"Someone stick Gary back in his cage," Sawyer called back to the guy.

"Only kidding!" Gary called to us. "Sawyer says you ladies cook!"

"We do," Jane called back to him, hitting a rim shot on the drums.

"This is Kimmy on lead, Sandra on bass, Savy on keyboards, and Jane on drums," Sawyer said, nodding at each of us. "They call themselves Wild Hearts." He grinned at me. "You're on, ladies!"

I felt a huge lump in my throat, and my hands were shaking, but when Savy counted us off for "Great Balls of Fire" I automatically began playing. I could see Sawyer bopping to the music, urging me on. When I felt confident enough to peek at the crowd, they seemed to be enjoying themselves. Savy's voice sounded great on lead. As we played I got less nervous, and I came in on all the right harmony parts. When we finished the song, everyone applauded and whistled, which made me feel more confident, per usual. After that, we did a new original of Jane's that we were planning to debut that Saturday at the school dance, a ballad called "Sleepless Nights." The crowd seemed to love that one. We finished with what we were all beginning to think of as our signature song, "It Wasn't God Who Made Honky Tonk Angels," done kind of rock with our three-part harmony. By the time we finished playing, sweat had made my T-shirt stick to my stomach so bad I figured it looked like Jim Morrison was taking a little nap there under my breasts. I discreetly turned around and pulled my T-shirt away from my body, then turned back as people began to surround us, telling us how good we were.

"That was great," Sawyer told me, giving me a quick kiss. On the lips. In front of everyone.

"Thanks," I replied, blushing happily.

"I have to go see about the food, so I'll

catch you in a few," he promised, and walked away.

"That boy looks good coming or going," I heard a cute curly-haired girl say as she watched Sawyer appreciatively.

Little thrills shot over me. Sawyer could have any girl in the world, but he wanted me. Me!

"I loved that arrangement of 'It Wasn't God Who Made Honky Tonk Angels,'" a pretty girl who looked to be in her early twenties told me. "The harmonies were awesome!"

"Thanks!" I said, feeling high and happy and even maybe a little confident. "Savy arranged it." I cocked my head at Savy, who was talking to a cute Asian guy in baggy shorts.

"And that country ballad, 'Sleepless Nights'—killer!" the girl continued enthusiastically.

I laughed. "Jane, our drummer, wrote it. Don't tell her you think it's country. She'll die!"

The pretty girl grinned. "Don't tell me: she hates country, right?"

"Right," I agreed.

"She thinks it's all oh-baby-you-stepped-on-me-and-did-me-wrong-but-I-still-love-you kind of junk, huh?"

I laughed. "Yeah, that sounds like Jane."

"Well, I'd love for her to hear some of my stuff sometime. I write country, but I don't write that crap! My name is Layne Schaefer, by the way," she added.

We shook hands.

"Do you think maybe ya'll could demo some of my stuff sometime?" Layne asked me. "Reba has a hold on one of my songs, and Suzy Bogguss has one I co-wrote on her next album."

"Wow, that's fantastic!" I told her.

"I'm trying." She shrugged.

"Hey, that guy just asked me if we could maybe demo some of his stuff!" Savy cried, running over to me. "He's a staff writer for Twang Twister Music. I am so psyched!"

"Savy, this is Layne," I said, introducing them. "Layne wants us to maybe demo some of her stuff, too. She's got a song on the next Suzy Bogguss album and—"

"Kimmy?"

I turned around.

Believe it or not, it was Dave Mallone.

Both of his eyes were circled with livid purple rings, and his nose was swathed in some kind of white packing.

"Dave ... what ... what are you doing here?" I whispered. "How long have you been here?" I smiled quickly at Layne, who was staring at Dave aghast. Well, no wonder. He looked like an accident victim.

"I was in the back of the crowd," Dave admitted. "I came to hear you play." His voice sounded funny because of his wrecked nose.

"How did you even know I would be here?" I asked him frantically.

"You told me," Dave replied.

This time I was sure he was lying. I hadn't even seen him since Wyatt had punched him out, which was the same day Sawyer invited Wild Hearts to play for his songwriters' meeting.

"I never told you," I insisted.

"Well, maybe Sawyer told me," he backtracked, blinking rapidly.

"I don't think so," I said. "I think you followed Sandra's Jeep here. Am I right?"

Dave just blinked.

"Am I right?" I demanded.

"I wanted to make sure you were okay."

"No, you didn't," I fumed. "Look, I've tried being nice to you, and I'm really sorry if you think there's something between us, but there isn't. And there never will be. So stop following me and stop calling me!" I was screaming by this time, but I just couldn't take it anymore.

"I never called you."

"Do you think I'm stupid?" I yelled. "All those phone calls where all you do is breathe?"

"I never did that!" Dave insisted, tears coming to his eyes.

"Oh, I guess not. You just follow me all over Nashville, lie to Sawyer and tell him we're an item, show up wherever I am—"

"But I'd do anything for you," Dave said in a low voice.

"Don't!" I cried. Dimly I realized a crowd was gathering, but I couldn't stop myself. "Don't do anything for me! Just stay away from me! Just get out of my face!"

I could hardly believe those things were coming out of my mouth, but it was as if I was yelling at my mother and my father and all the girls at school who had laughed at my stupid cutoff jean skirt. For a moment—just a brief moment—I had a rush of triumph because I felt big and someone else felt little.

Dave staggered as if I had hit him, and then he ran out of the studio.

Which was just about the moment I began to hate myself for being so awful. So I started after him.

"Kimmy, don't," Sandra said, putting her hand on my arm.

"But I was so hateful—"

"I know you feel bad," Sandra said, "but if

you go after him you'll just encourage him again. You can't keep giving him mixed signals or he'll never leave you alone."

"Serious cretin," Jane commented.

I put my face in my hands. "God, I was so mean to him."

"He's got major problems, Kimmy," Savy said. "You can't make them your problems."

"I think the current cool term is co-dependent," Jane said helpfully, lifting her hair off the back of her neck to fan herself.

"Your boyfriend?" Layne asked me.

"No!" I practically screamed. "He is not my boyfriend!"

"Hey, I was just asking," Layne said, taking a step backwards.

"I'm sorry," I mumbled. "It's just that—"

"Yo, chow time!" Gary bellowed from the front door of the studio. "Get it while it's hot!"

Everyone headed en masse out the front door and crossed the lawn to the sliding glass doors at the back of Sawyer's huge house. Even though the last thing I felt was hungry I dutifully followed along until we came to a huge room where a buffet of chili, salad, and cold cuts was laid out on a long table.

"Wait until you taste Yolanda's chili," Sawyer said, coming over to put his arm around me. "It'll put hair on your chest."

"She's already got tons of that," Jane called over her shoulder as she headed for the chili line. "We mow her on a regular basis."

Sawyer cocked his head at me. "You okay?"

I don't know why, but I didn't even want to go into the Dave fiasco with him. I suppose it embarrassed me.

So I just said I was okay, and Sawyer got me some chili, which I tried to eat. A couple of other people came over to tell me how good Wild Hearts sounded and to ask if maybe we'd demo some of their stuff.

Sawyer sat with me on the couch, his arm around me. It felt so wonderful. Soon I stopped worrying about Dave. My friends were right. Dave had to take care of his own problems.

Besides, I wasn't a geek like him anymore. My life was changing. Dave would have to change his own life.

Someone put a Wylie and the Wild West Show tape on really loud, and the noise of the party escalated over the music. I saw Savy in the corner with the cute Asian guy again, and Sandra and Jane were sitting with two guys on the other side of the room, laughing hysterically. Occasionally Sawyer's hand slid under my hair to massage my neck. I was in heaven.

I remember someone was telling a story about Lee Greenwood flirting with some girls backstage at the Opry, and then the CD that was playing ended, and I looked up, and there was Dave again, standing in the middle of the room.

With a gun.

Pointed at me.

It didn't seem real.

"That guy has a gun!" someone shrieked.

Someone else screamed, and the news spread through the room like wildfire. Everyone moved away from Dave.

Silence.

"How could you?" Dave whispered to me, his face a mask of misery.

"Dave, don't—" I managed.

"How could you do it to me?" Dave continued. "I loved you! And all you did was humiliate me in front of everyone!"

Very, very slowly Sawyer stood up. "Come on, now, Dave," Sawyer said. "You don't want to do this."

"Shut up!" Dave cried, pointing the gun at Sawyer.

"I'm cool, buddy," Sawyer said, holding his hands up to Dave. "I'm not moving."

Dave turned the gun back to me. "You want to know how it feels, to love someone and have them laugh at you in front of everyone?"

"But I didn't—"

"Weenie Mallone, Dave the Geek!" Dave cried. "You think that doesn't hurt? You think I don't have any feelings?"

"But, Dave, I never called you those things," I said softly.

"You thought them," Dave replied bitterly. "But you don't feel so cool now, do you?" he asked me. He whirled around, pointing the gun haphazardly around the room, and people jumped back. "Do you?" he yelled at the crowd.

Savy made a move toward me, and Dave whirled around, pointing the gun at her. "If anyone in this room moves again, it will be Kimmy's fault. I'll kill her and then Sawyer and then myself. I mean it."

"Dave, Kimmy's your friend," Sawyer said slowly, taking a small step toward Dave. He let his hand rest lightly on the coffee table. Sawyer's eyes flicked to mine and then back to the table, as if he wanted me to notice something. I looked over at his hand on the table, and he slowly pressed down on a small metal bar just under the table. Dave's eyes were back on me, and I hoped—I prayed—that Sawyer had just set off some kind of an alarm.

"This is your fault. You know that, don't you?" Dave asked me.

"No, Dave—"

"Yes!" He held the gun out at me and then at Sawyer. "Don't you move. Don't either of you move."

"You know, you have more friends than you realize," Sawyer said.

"Bull," Dave snapped. "Do you think I'm stupid? Did you ever once have a conversation with me at school?"

"Well, we did that science project together," Sawyer reminded Dave. "Remember that? It was great. On the atom?"

At first I thought Sawyer was crazy, talking to Dave about a science project. But then I remembered the little bar on the table. Maybe, just maybe, Sawyer had called the police and he was trying to keep Dave talking until they showed up.

"You two won some kind of prize for that, didn't you?" I asked Dave.

"A science prize," Dave snorted. "Perfect for Weenie Mallone, huh?"

"I never did understand half of your research," Sawyer continued. "I mean, it was way over my head."

"It was easy," Dave insisted. "Splitting atoms, that's all."

"I don't even really know what an atom is," I said.

"Atoms are the particles that make up a molecule," Dave said. "Big duh."

I shrugged. "I don't get it."

So Dave started talking about atoms, all the time pointing that gun at me and Sawyer. No one else dared to move. He was ranting about science, hurling everything he knew at us about atoms and quarks and black holes in space.

"Probably none of you even understand about black holes," Dave ranted. "You're too busy worrying about football games and popularity contests. You're too busy making me feel like dirt. Well, who feels like dirt now? Huh? Huh?"

Behind Dave I saw two men in blue uniforms enter the room ever so quietly. But Dave had his eyes on mine, and he saw my eyes flicker, so he whirled around.

"Put the gun down, son," the older cop said, his hand on his own gun.

Dave gave a strangled cry and turned on me, there was a loud shot, I screamed. Next to me Sawyer fell back on to the couch, a shocked look on his face, blood seeping through his T-shirt.

Oh, my God. Oh, my God.

Dave had shot Sawyer.

"Kimmy?" Sawyer said, his expression quizzical.

"Oh, God!" I screamed, clapping my hand over my mouth.

Sawyer moaned my name again, the cops grabbed Dave, everyone went crazy screaming, crying.

One cop put a call through on his walkie-talkie while the other handcuffed Dave. I knelt by Sawyer, tears streaming down my face.

"Oh, Sawyer, oh, God," I whispered. I put my hand over his T-shirt where the blood was gushing out.

"Help him!" I screamed at the cop. "Help him!"

"Move away, miss," the younger cop said sternly. He knelt by Sawyer and began to administer first aid.

Savy pulled me away, and I turned my head into her chest, sobbing my guts out.

This kind of thing only happened in the movies or in really bad neighborhoods. It didn't happen to me or to anyone I knew. It had to be a nightmare.

But it wasn't. It was real.

In the distance I heard the eerie wail of an ambulance coming closer, coming for Sawyer.

And all I could think was *Please, dear God, don't let Sawyer die.*

CHAPTER
12

❤

"It's my fault," I said.

Savy, Jane, and Sandra sat with me in the waiting area at St. Thomas Hospital, where they'd taken Sawyer. We'd been there for hours, while Sawyer was in surgery. After giving statements to the police, we'd all come to the hospital to wait and see how Sawyer was. I felt so sick, like fainting or throwing up. It was like some terrible nightmare, only it was really happening.

"It's not your fault," Sandra insisted. "You didn't pull a gun on Sawyer and you didn't shoot. Dave did."

Tears came to my eyes for what felt like the zillionth time in the last few hours. "Yes, but Dave was aiming for me," I reminded Sandra. "Sawyer didn't do anything."

"Well, neither did you," Savy said firmly. She reached up and put one of her short arms around my wide shoulders.

I wiped the tears off my face with the back of my fist. "That's right, I didn't," I agreed bitterly. "Dave has been sick for a long time—I can see that now—and I didn't do anything at all. I just worried about myself, about how he was embarrassing me—"

"Kimmy, gimme a break!" Jane cried. "Dave just terrorized a whole group of people. Then he shot someone! He should go to prison and rot, and I hope he does!"

"How can you say that?" I exploded. "He's sick! He's not a criminal!"

"If everyone in New York who was sick wasn't considered a criminal, all of the Looney Tunes would be out on the street and the prisons would be empty," Jane replied.

"This isn't New York," I said.

"There are sickos everywhere," Jane pointed out.

"You can't hold yourself responsible for what he did," Savy said earnestly.

"But I *am* responsible," I said. "I *feel* responsible."

"How about his parents? And his guidance counselors? And everyone else who knows him?" Sandra asked. "Why put the blame on your shoulders?"

I felt the hot tears forming again. "Because I told him we were friends. I'm just a liar, a shallow, stupid liar—"

"You're not!" Savy insisted.

"I am. All I cared about was getting Sawyer to like me. All I wanted was to change my image, to be someone other than boring scared-of-my-own-shadow me." I caught a reflection of myself in the glass near the nurses' station. Mascara had run down my face, my hair was a mess, my new Jim Morrison T-shirt was bloody. "If Sawyer . . . lives . . . he's going to hate me, and he should. I hate myself."

"No, Kimmy—" Savy began.

"Yes," I managed in between sobs. "My mother was right. I disgust myself. I'm trying to be someone I'm not. None of this would have happened if I hadn't tried to be in the band."

I saw Jane, Savy, and Sandra exchange looks, but I didn't care. It was all over. I only wished I could go back to the way my life was before. So what if it was boring? So what if I'd never been out on a date and never been kissed? And so what if no one knew I could play the guitar? This wasn't better. Not at all.

"You don't really mean that," Jane finally said. "About Wild Hearts."

"I do," I said flatly. "You can find another guitar player. It's over."

No one said anything. I knew I was letting everybody down, but I felt too awful to care. Sawyer was in surgery right that moment, all because of me. Telling my friends they had to find a new guitar player seemed like small potatoes in comparison.

"Is there a Kimmy Carrier out here?" a middle-aged doctor in hospital scrubs asked from the doorway of the waiting room.

I jumped up. "Me," I said and hurried over to him.

"I'm Dr. Abrams," he said, shaking my hand. "Sawyer was able to give us your name right before he went into surgery."

"Yes?" I said faintly, clenching my hands so hard that my fingernails made ridges in my skin.

"Sawyer came through the surgery well—"

"Oh, thank God!" I cried, grabbing the doctor's hand.

"It's not all good news, I'm afraid," the doctor continued gently. "The bullet badly injured one lung, and Sawyer's other lung is not taking over as well as it should. We've got him on a respirator."

I clapped a hand over my mouth.

"I know it sounds frightening, but we hope that this is only temporary," Dr. Abrams continued.

"Is he . . . will he—"

"He's in critical but stable condition at the moment," Dr. Abrams said.

I gulped hard. "Does his family know?"

"We were able to get his parents' permission for the surgery. We reached them on the mobile phone in his father's tour bus. His parents are on their way back here now from Indianapolis."

"Can I see him?" I asked.

"He's not awake now," Dr. Abrams said. "He can't have any visitors yet anyway, except his parents when they arrive."

"I understand," I whispered, even though I desperately wanted to see him, if only to look at his face, if only to whisper how sorry I was.

"He did manage to give me a message for you before he went into surgery," Dr. Abrams continued.

I just stared at him, my eyes swimming with tears.

"He said, 'Tell Kimmy I love her,' " Dr. Abrams reported, a kind look on his face.

My mouth fell open. "He did?"

The doctor nodded.

I grabbed his hand. "Say it again," I begged.

"Sawyer said, 'Tell Kimmy I love her,'" Dr. Abrams repeated.

"Oh, thank you, thank you so much, and thank you for taking care of him and everything," I babbled.

"He's a brave young man," the doctor told me. "He's strong and he's healthy. There's every reason for us to be optimistic."

I went back to my friends, who were waiting with terrorized looks on their faces. They were holding their breath.

"He's alive," I told them first.

They all let air whoosh out of their mouths. Then I told them everything else medical that I knew.

"So this respirator thing is temporary?" Jane asked nervously.

"The doctor didn't say for sure," I replied. "I don't think he knows."

I sat down next to Savy. "One other thing the doctor told me. Something Sawyer said before he went into surgery. He ... he said he loves me."

"Oh, Kimmy," Savy said, squeezing my hand.

"I can't believe it," I admitted, "but I don't think the doctor would make that up."

"Believe it," Sandra assured me firmly.

"But . . . but how can he love me?" I asked my friends. "How can it be possible?"

"Because he knows you're not responsible, even if you don't," Jane pointed out. She gave me a caring smile. "I told you it meant something when he kissed you."

I smiled back, but the smile quickly left my lips. I had no right to feel good about anything, not with Dave in jail and Sawyer so badly injured.

"Can you see him?" Savy asked me.

I shook my head no. "His parents are on their way back from Indianapolis. They should be here soon and—"

At that moment Sawyer's parents hurried across the waiting room. I would have recognized his father anywhere, he was that famous. Sawyer looked exactly like his dad, only with darker hair. His mother was a beautiful slender blonde, though at the moment she looked the way I felt—terrified.

Sawyer's dad asked the nurse where his son was, and she said she'd call the doctor. Then he and Mrs. Paxton paced in front of the nurses' station. I gathered up my courage and walked over to them.

"Excuse me. I'm Kimmy Carrier, a friend of Sawyer's," I told them.

"He mentioned you," his father said, lines

of anxiety etched around his eyes. "You're the guitar player, right?"

I nodded, surprised that Sawyer had said anything about me to his parents.

"Have you seen him?" his mother asked, biting on her lower lip.

"No."

"But he's—"

"He came through surgery fine, the doctor told me," I said gently.

Mr. Paxton ran his hands through his hair. "How the hell did this happen? How did my son get shot? At our home, for chrissakes!"

"It was a . . . a friend of mine," I said in a low voice. I felt I had to say that, I don't know why. "He meant to shoot me."

Sawyer's mother's eyes grew round. "You mean to tell me that Sawyer was shot because of a fight between you and your boyfriend?"

"Oh, no!" I cried quickly. "Not my boyfriend, he's—"

"It's your fault, then!" she continued, oblivious of my attempts to explain.

"Come on, Janette," Mr. Paxton chided gently, putting a hand on her arm. "We don't know that."

"Yes, we do. This girl just said so!" Sawyer's mother insisted. She whirled back on me. "If anything happens to my baby, I will never forgive you. Do you hear me?"

I took a step back as if she'd hit me.

"Please, my wife is just upset. She doesn't know what she's saying," Judd Paxton told me.

But I already felt so guilty that it was as if Sawyer's mother was just saying the truth I already knew. "I'm so sorry . . ."

Mrs. Paxton put her head in her hands and sobbed as her husband put his arms around her. I backed away slowly and walked over to my friends.

"We heard," Sandra said curtly. "Let's get out of here."

"How can I leave Sawyer?" I whispered.

"Look, you can't see him, and you can't help him right now," Jane said. "And his mom is so crazed that it'll be better if you're not around."

"I'll leave my phone number with the nurse," Savy offered, and she went over to the nurses' station.

My friends led me out to Sandra's Jeep, and we drove to Savy's house. Jane and Sandra both called home and said they were staying over at Savy's house. Savy had called home earlier from the hospital so her family would know where we were—she'd called my parents, too, since I was too upset to do it—and now everyone was asleep except Gramma Beth, who was sitting in the kitchen, drinking chamomile tea.

She took one look at me and held out her arms, and I fell into them gratefully, sobbing my heart out.

"It's okay, little one," Gramma Beth crooned to me. "You go ahead and cry." As she held me she lifted her head to talk to Savy. "Run up and tell your parents you're okay. I made them go to bed, but I promised you'd stop in when you got home."

Savy kissed her grandmother and ran upstairs to see her parents, and something about that made me start sobbing all over again. No one was waiting up for me to see how I was. My parents only seemed to care if they thought I might get kidnapped. It was like an ache in my heart, that loneliness.

When I felt as if I had no more tears left inside me, I sat down at the big kitchen table. Gramma Beth brought us a platter of her homemade raisin-oatmeal cookies and some tea.

"Oh, Gramma Beth, you think eating cures everything," Savy told her grandmother lovingly when she came back downstairs.

"It couldn't hurt," Gramma Beth said with a shrug. She sat down with us and folded her arms. "So, how is the boy?"

We told her what we knew.

She nodded. "So now we pray and we wait and see."

I put my forehead down on my hands. "I don't think God answers prayers, Gramma Beth."

"No?" she asked me.

"No. I don't think God can be petitioned."

"I don't think so either," she agreed. "But I do think that something changes when people—enough people—pray for a good thing. It just doesn't always happen in ways we can understand."

Everyone sat silently drinking tea, and I excused myself and went up to Savy's room. It was a mess—her room was always a mess—and I stepped over discarded clothes, CDs, books, and a half-eaten sandwich and made my way into her bathroom. I dropped my clothes on the floor and stepped into the shower, running the water so hot that my skin turned lobster red the instant the needles of water hit it. I welcomed the pain. I scrubbed off what was left of my makeup, and then I scrubbed my whole self over and over. But no matter how much I washed, I didn't feel clean.

I had just wrapped myself up in a terry-cloth robe of Savy's that barely came to my thighs when my friends came into the room.

"We were wondering what happened to

you," Jane said, throwing a jacket off the bed so she could sit down.

"Do you feel better?" Savy asked me.

I sat on the bed and huddled in her robe. "Not really." I took a deep breath. "Listen, I want ya'll to know I was serious about dropping out of the band."

"Don't make that decision now," Jane said. "It doesn't make any sense to—"

"I don't care," I interrupted her. "Nothing makes any sense anymore, does it? Ya'll have to find a new lead guitar player."

"But we want you!" Savy cried passionately.

"Because I'm a good guitar player," I said. "Well, there are other guitar players."

"Look, will you at least stay in the band until we find a replacement?" Jane asked.

I nodded. "But you need to start looking right away. I want out as soon as I can get out."

"Why?" Sandra asked me.

I stared at her. "How can you ask me that?"

"Dropping out of the band isn't going to change anything," Sandra remarked. "You can't . . . I don't know . . . punish yourself into making things better."

"That's not what I'm doing," I said flatly.

"This is a dumb time for you to decide

something like this!" Jane insisted. "Give yourself some time to—"

The phone by Savy's bed rang, startling me so much that I practically jumped off the bed. I caught a quick glimpse of the clock on her night table. It was two o'clock in the morning.

It could only mean one thing.

R-i-i-i-ng! R-i-i-i-ng!

I stared at Savy, she stared at me, then finally she reached for the phone.

"Hello? Yes, she's here. Just a moment." She handed me the receiver.

"Hello?" I said.

"This is Mr. Paxton calling, Sawyer's dad."

I gulped hard and held the receiver so tight my knuckles turned white. "Yes?"

"I wanted to let you know that Sawyer was taken off the respirator a little while ago," Mr. Paxton said.

"Is he—"

"He's much better," Mr. Paxton assured me. "His other lung is doing well. The doctor has upgraded his condition. I thought you'd want to know."

"Oh, thank you. Thank you so much for calling me!" I cried.

"You're welcome," Mr. Paxton said. "Please don't pay any mind to what my wife said. Understand, she's just distraught."

"I do," I assured him.

"Sawyer can't really talk yet, from that big ole tube having been down his throat, but he managed to squiggle your name on a sheet of paper. I figured that meant my boy thinks you're pretty danged special."

"Thank you, Mr. Paxton." I hung up and turned to my friends. Now silent tears of happiness were cascading down my cheeks. "Sawyer's off the respirator," I told them, grinning happily. "He's going to be okay!"

Savy, Jane, and Sandra all came rushing over to me, hugging me, laughing and crying at the same time.

"Maybe Gramma Beth is right!" Savy said, wiping the tears from her cheeks. "Because I've been praying as hard as I could."

"And now that we know Sawyer's okay, you don't have to quit the band!" Jane added.

"That hasn't changed," I insisted. "That's not why I'm quitting."

"I don't understand," Savy said. "I thought—"

"Don't you see?" I said earnestly. "I was turning into someone else—someone I don't even like. I was worrying about all the wrong things—stupid things like how cool I looked and how popular I was. That's not the kind of person I want to be!"

"But you're confusing two different things," Sandra insisted. "You don't have to be shallow to play lead guitar in Wild Hearts. It just doesn't follow."

"Ya'll can find someone else," I insisted.

"Don't you understand?" Jane said, her hands on her hips. "It isn't just the music. It's you, you idiot. We want you!"

"Really?" I asked in a small voice.

"Jeez, let's put it on a billboard and drive her past it," Sandra snorted.

I fiddled with the sash of Savy's robe. "I don't know," I finally said. "But I ... I need some time to figure things out. I've got to go see Dave. I've got to talk to him, spend some time with him—"

"In prison?" Jane asked, her eyebrows raised.

"His parents will put up bail, I bet," Sandra guessed.

"I know his parents are rich. I remember he told me that once," I said. "But he lives with some aunt or something—I don't know why. He told me he hates his parents, and he thinks they hate him."

"Cold," Savy commented.

"Well, anyway, he'll have a trial," Sandra said. "He's not going to go to jail for a while, if he goes at all."

"In the meantime, he's going to need a friend," I said firmly.

Jane shook her head and threw Savy's stuffed panda at me. "I really do not understand you, Kimmy."

"Well, I don't much understand me, either," I said, patting the bear's furry ears.

"You know Sawyer will want you to stay in the band," Savy pointed out.

"Maybe," I agreed. "But I can't do it for him, any more than I can do it for you, Savy." I looked over at her. "I have to figure out what I want to do for myself." I gave her a tremulous smile. "Do you hate me?"

"Oh, Kimmy, I could never hate you," Savy said earnestly. "You're my best friend, and you always will be!"

"Jane?" I asked, looking at her.

"Well, you're not my best friend," Jane said. "Music is my best friend." She grumbled and sighed heavily. "But you guys come in a close second."

"Sandra?" I asked her.

"Kimmy, you do what you gotta do," she said. "It looks like you might just have some backbone after all."

Wow. So maybe Jane and Sandra really did like me. A little. Maybe more than a little.

"Thanks," I told them fervently.

"We're not giving up on trying to talk you into staying in the band, you know," Savy said. "Just consider yourself warned." She stood up and pulled off her T-shirt, dropping her clothes all over the room, per usual. "I'm beat. Do ya'll want to sleep over?"

"I'm definitely too tired to drive home," Sandra said.

"As much as I'd enjoy scaring the life out of my little sister by walking in at three in the morning, I guess I'll stay, too," Jane agreed.

"Only cuz you don't have a ride home without Sandra," Savy pointed out with a laugh.

Savy handed Jane and Sandra oversized T-shirts and slipped into one herself. They were all too whipped to even shower, so Jane crawled into a sleeping bag that Savy pulled out of her closet, and Sandra curled up on the small couch in the corner. Savy and I got into her bed, and we turned out the lights.

There in the dark I thought about how lucky I was to have friends like Savy, Jane, and Sandra. I thought about Sawyer, who had actually told the doctor that he loved me! And I thought about how awful it was for Dave, who didn't have anyone who really cared about him at all. The world was just too cold and lonely and scary that way. So maybe I didn't have the greatest parents in the world. Maybe I just had the greatest friends.

"I love you guys," I whispered into the dark.

"Shut up, Kimmy. I was just falling asleep," Jane groused.

"This couch has lumps," Sandra added.

"We love you, too, Kimmy," Savy said, rolling over.

I smiled up at the ceiling.

Because I actually, finally really believed that it was true.

Dear Readers,

Woah baby and yowza, have you guys ever responded to WILD HEARTS!! I'm so glad because I love writing this series and I want it to go on forever! My dream in high school was to have my own band, but (sob) it never happened. So now I get to live out all my fantasies through the incredibly cool girls in WILD HEARTS.

Life update: I am soooo busy. I'm writing lotsa books, two screenplays, and am trying to find the time to write a new play based on one of my novels. My husband, Jeff (Hi, honey), and I go back and forth to Los Angeles a lot, working on various TV and film deals. And speaking of TV and movies, what do you guys watch? Do you think teen stuff on TV and in the movies could be improved? What would you like to see?

So, listen, if any of you are ever gonna be in Nashville, write and let me know. We should meet, don't you think? I love meeting my readers—I learn so much from you guys! I do travel and make appearances at schools and bookstores, so watch the paper in case I'm coming to your town.

I really want to thank you so much for reading WILD HEARTS. I really want to hear all your ideas so that I can make this series exactly what you want it to be. One of the best parts about writing teen books is hearing from people like you. I answer each and every letter I receive personally, so if you write to me I will definitely write you back! Also, I'll be picking letters to appear here in "Heart-to-Heart," so do let me know if it's okay to consider your letter for publication. If I pick your letter, you'll receive a free autographed copy of the book in which your letter appears. And if your letter is personal, just say so. You can trust that no one will see it but me, I promise.

Thanks again for being such a huge part of my work. You're terrific!

Wild Hearts Forever!

Cherie Bennett

Cherie Bennett
c/o Archway Paperbacks
Pocket Books
1230 Avenue of the Americas
New York, NY 10020

Heart to Heart
~ ♥ ♥ ~

Dear Cherie,

I thought your newest novel, WILD HEARTS, was excellent. I couldn't put it down. The book was four things: realistic, touching, spellbinding, and most of all, exquisite. I hope Kimmy is able to finally develop self-confidence, and I wish Sandra would allow people to see more of her soul. Even perfect people have problems! Is the series going to be just four books—one for each girl—or endless (I hope!!), like SUNSET ISLAND?

> *Much love and luck,*
> *Chali Thakrar*
> *Tipton, Indiana*

Dear Chali,

You're right. Even "perfect" people do have problems! I remember when I found out that the girl at my high school who seemed to have everything (you know the type—looks, brains, talent, cool boyfriend) was actually an alcoholic. Her family life was so messed up that she tried to kill herself. But she hid all of this from everyone at school. You will certainly be finding out more about Sandra and who she really is, especially in Book #4, WILD HEARTS ON THE EDGE. And yes, Chali, I'm happy to say that WILD HEARTS will go on and on . . . by popular demand! Thanks!!

> Best,
> Cherie

Dear Cherie,

*Hello! I have read all your SUNSET ISLAND books
and was so excited to read WILD HEARTS. I loved
it! You touched base on real issues such as almost being
raped, drunk-driving, low self-esteem, consequences of
drunk-driving, and the feeling of not belonging. I think
it's great that Jane wants to be her own woman, and
not resort to being one of the "pastel people." Your
books are the only ones I read that aren't horror!*

> *Love always,*
> *Dawn Robinson*
> *Boca Raton, Florida*

Dear Dawn,

I'm certainly glad you mentioned the dreaded
"pastel people!" There was certainly a group like
that at my high school. How about yours? Very
scary, if you ask me! Anyway, thanks for saying
I rank up there with horror writers. But I gotta
ask you, what is the deal with the lust for horror,
anyway? I really would like to know. All of you
horror lovers out there, puh-leez write and tell
me the appeal!

> Best,
> Cherie

Dear Cherie,

I loved your new book, WILD HEARTS. It shows how hard it is to move to a new place and start all over again. Jane is a little bit like my sister. We moved to Nashville after living in a small town in Missouri. She hated country music, but eventually she learned to listen and hear what it says. I just have to say I love your writing and I can really relate to the circumstances you write about. Please keep writing. You put me in a good mood and make me laugh.

> *Love you always,*
> *Dawn Lyndon*
> *Nashville, Tennessee*

Dear Dawn,

I love to make people laugh, so thanks for the compliment! I think Jane may turn out to have a lot in common with your sister, since she's now in a country-rock band! So, what do all of you out there think of country music? As most of you know, I grew up a die-hard rocker, but now I listen to country more than I listen to rock. The best of country is poetry about real life. Of course, the worst of it deserves to go out to sea on a retch raft, but that's not the stuff I listen to! I'm a huge fan of Garth Brooks (not to brag, but I know the guy since I've worked with him), Mary-Chapin Carpenter and Pam Tillis (check out her song "Let that Pony Run" if you wanna hear greatness!).

> Best,
> Cherie

Get a WILD HEARTS Magnet...*FREE!*

Of course you're wild about Cherie Bennett's hot new series *WILD HEARTS!* Now you can get a *free* WILD HEARTS magnet that will look *great* in your locker by:

- filling in the coupon below,
- clipping the half-a-heart from WILD HEARTS and the half from WILD HEARTS ON FIRE (on sale mid-March, 1994) *and*
- mailing all three to:

   Pocket Books
   Dept. WH, 13th Floor
   1230 Ave of the Americas
   New York, NY 10020

Name (please print clearly)   Birthdate

Street Address

City   State   Zip

No electronically reproduced copies will be accepted. Offer good only in the U.S. and Canada while supplies last. The first one thousand respondents who properly submit the requested materials will be mailed a free magnet. One to a customer, please.